The Modern Age

Jane Covernton

The Modern Age

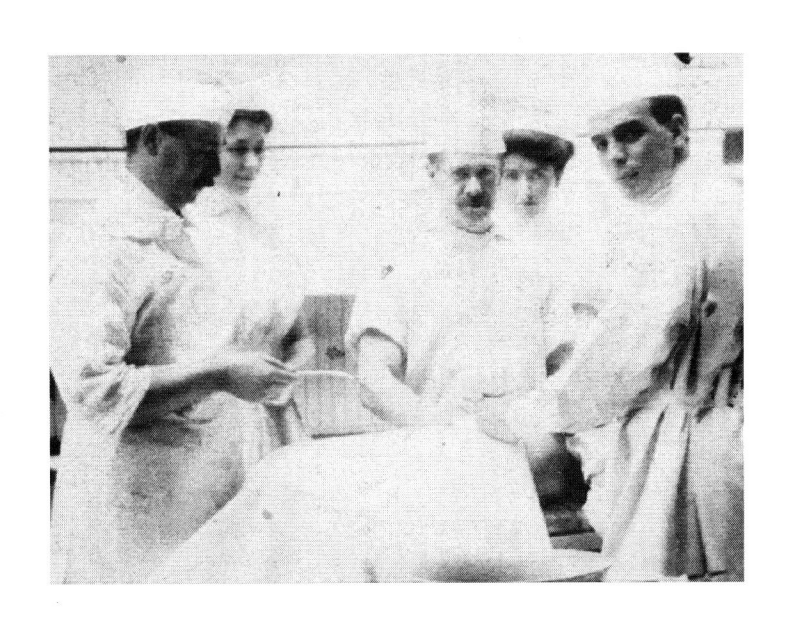

Calendula Farms

Library and Archives Canada Cataloguing in Publication

Covernton, Jane, 1949-
      The modern age / Jane Covernton.

ISBN 978-0-9682477-1-6

      I. Title.

PS8555.O8524M63 2010   C813'.54
C2010-901475-8

Published by Calendula Farms,
Box 193,
Roberts Creek, British Columbia, Canada
V0N 2W0
jcovernton@gmail.com
www.janecovernton.ca
This is a work of fiction. Any resemblance to persons living or dead is purely coincidental.

This book is dedicated to the memory of Ruthie Van Kleek, who lost her husband in the last days of the First World War, who was a school teacher, a good friend, a reader, and an exemplar of the art of growing old.

And, as usual with great gratitude, to John Gibbs.

ONE

Last night I woke again with all the warm sleep drained away without my noticing, and my body lying chilled, in consciousness again. I was dreaming I was looking at photographs of us all – Zoë and I in long dresses, then shorter during the War, the padded shoulders of my work life in the forties, cocktail dresses, and now me, old, in the pants I only ever wear.

In some ways my life has been one damn thing after another. I need to tell a thing or two and I'm too old to care anymore about the proprieties. So I decided then, last night, lying sleepless for so long, to try to write this, to tell a story about Zoë and me because I just can't stop thinking and it's so

The Modern Age

uncomfortable. I feel so wrong and regretful. Nothing about Zoë's story feels fair and I keep thinking, and sometimes muttering (out loud to my dismay): Why? Why? So I'll tell it. Who it is I'm telling I don't know, but there it is, this need that comes on me in the middle of the night and will not let me be.

Actually this story starts from two different places. Aside from this pull of sadness about Zoë, there's another more official story I might or might not tell. I've been asked by Dr. Robinson at the Medical Society to write about how I became a doctor, about how it was for women becoming doctors in the early years of this century. I said no, then yes. That was several days ago. Maybe that's what's keeping me awake now still. It's been difficult to get started. So many other things seem to hang around that little story, weighing it down. Or to put it another way, that one official story seems pregnant with the sadness of the other. They offered to send out a young woman with a tape recorder to interview me, but I trust that even less. So just start, I say to myself, and let the other story leak out or get born or whatever.

I suppose it must be for the girls: Zoë's story, written for her granddaughters, my great-nieces, or great-great, whatever they are, Penny and Sarah, so that they don't forget how it was and don't have to do it all again. Or something like that. I don't suppose anyone will care particularly.

Penny gave me this book for Christmas, about housewives and their thwarted lives. Or women generally and their thwarted lives. Maybe that's what's got me all stirred up, some kind of spiritual indigestion keeping me awake. Penny wants something from me but I can't tell quite what. The book is all the rage apparently in her intellectual circles. Penny's an academic, unmarried at twenty-seven, going for her doctorate in history, beetle-browed and fiercely independent. Her twin, Sarah, is the opposite, married, with two little children, living in a house near here in Kerrisdale. What does Penny want from me? Well I was never a housewife. Anyway I started out to write about Zoë.

Zoë never got to "be" anything and I was a "lady doctor", one of those "male men lady doctors" they talked about, and yet I feel it was Zoë who was the New Woman and I the Old. My sorrow is that we never got to see about her, what her paintings would have been like, or what if she had started doing sculpture as she wanted to? And what really keeps me awake at night is the idea that it was my fault about her death. I feel a very bad person. I should have been able to keep her alive somehow.

This was Zoë: painting under a cliff, waist deep in water, dazzled by sunlight, utterly absorbed, didn't know one meal from another. Why do we have to keep on proving it? It what? Proving we had a right to be fully alive. Something like that.

The problem, I can see right away, is that it's difficult for me to remember when things happened and the order in which they happened. I can't remember so well what I had for dinner last night, but the past is vivid, increasingly vivid, coming back in large brightly lit and even scented scenes. This morning came the time I ran through a patch of nettles, brushed my bare legs. There was a sharp fresh green smell then my legs tingled with pain. Someone, a gardener perhaps, or one of the servants, stepped out of the cottonwoods and pressed a leaf in my hand then rubbed it on the burning skin. The pain eased, the skin still tingled, the mysterious man disappeared. How old was I? I don't know. Perhaps four. Who was the man? I don't know.

This is how it comes to me, unbidden, the past with no explanation. Often with no words. Just flashes of feeling. Some things I can remember quite clearly: fifteen years old, muffled in fabric, walking in winter in London, holding a muff to my face, blood warm, in love with Hugo and full of suppressed desire. That's vivid enough. I don't want to write about Hugo though.

When it comes to events and ordering a telling, it's hard to remember what came first, how things unfolded. However,

The Modern Age

certain solid dates are like lampposts shining their light all around. 1900: the New Year's Eve party at the beginning of this century, the night Zoë's parents, my half-brother and his wife, died. 1907: the stock crash that wiped out our fortune, sent Cornelius off a bridge, and brought Zoë into early labour and Morgan into our lives. 1914: the War started and a day soon after that, Zoë walked into a dark river and drowned. All the violent events have dates. The day Morgan was taken away from me: March 15, 1915. The long peaceful times of loving and practicing are blurred. Such as they were.

Then there are the mysteries I can't seem to let go. My mind still rampages through the past, as I rampaged through Susannah's papers when she died, trying to figure out, to find a clue to the question: who was Zoë's lover, Morgan's father? Perhaps I should put Penny on the case. She's a rampager herself. And why did Hugo leave me? But this is not about that.

I'm eighty-five years old now. The New Year is 1964. Where did the time go? I'm an old woman lying in the cold bath of memories, shaking my head back and forth like a dog with water in the ear, shaking with regret. My own little dog pushes her body hard against my legs to get petted. She's amazingly strong for a little thing. Her tail brushes silky against my dry old legs. I open curtains. This day looks good. Trees burst into silver flames across the street in the early slanting winter light. Red poinsettia plants here on the mahogany are almost dead, yet still glow. Why do I shrink from life, why am I anxious so much of the time, afraid to go out, afraid of death?

An interruption: Morgan has phoned. He and his wife are coming to tea. I'm afraid that I'm in for one of their lectures. He was formal, calling me Mary-Margaret instead of Aunt Em. I know what he wants: to curtail my freedom in some way. Or perhaps what she wants. Why can't I remember her name, his wife? It's hard enough to deal with this apparently pressing need for organized recollection without having to worry about what they want. Try to stay focused.

The Modern Age

The story: My mother died. I was a child. I can feel myself sinking back into that. Then Zoë came along. This will be the story of hysteria, of Zoë's hysteria, the whole family's hysteria. Think of the pattern a flower makes in the world, in time. Hysteria flowers, spreads like a weed. It's contagious. Bindweed climbing over the garden of neglect, the white flower opening and going to seed and white roots running everywhere. Hysteria flowers and the whole family catch it. I close my eyes for a moment and remember, or see: books, dust, sneezing, a big apron, smudged and dirty. A pale servant. That should be enough to get me started.

But perhaps I'm too old for this after all, not enough life left to do this. Well, I still enjoy swimming, the feel of seaweed against my ancient legs. They're so wrinkled and loose, so bloodless, that barnacle cuts on my thighs don't even draw blood. I still love to swim, against the amusement of all those on the beach. That was last summer anyway. Perhaps I have enough energy left to peck out this tale on my old Remington.

Just start.

1880, the year I was born, Ibsen's outrageous play, A Doll's House, opened in Copenhagen. Five years later, the horseless carriage was invented. My name could have been Violet, Constance, Faith. Those were the times for names like that. But it was Mary-Margaret. I kept the same name throughout my life: Mary-Margaret Martin Howard, except for when I was briefly, but vividly, Martin.

The night I was born, there was an ice storm. Layers of freezing rain caked the trees of Montreal. Sparkling branches cracked and then crashed into icy streets. My father, used to walking everywhere, almost killed himself getting back to the hospital. So the family story goes.

I was born in the Royal Victoria Hospital in Montreal, Canada. We lived in Mount Royal: wealthy, Protestant, English, with the French below in the city and countryside around, poor and Catholic. We lived in a stone house with a garden drifting down the hillside alongside a stone stairway.

Living in our house was like living inside a magic tree with shiny dark wood everywhere. A wood-paneled staircase came down into a large dark hallway and stopped beside a bronze statue of a shepherd girl. I remember the feel of the smooth cool skin of her green metal arm. My favourite place was the seat in the window half way down the stairs, looking out over the garden and down into the city. The seat was padded and covered in bright red paisley swirls that I traced with my fingers. My mother's clothing swished on the stairs alerting me to her gentle presence. There was so much more to clothing then. I remember a sense of safety.

Over the years, I've been an enthusiastic supporter of dress reform and my own homes have been simple and even spare compared to the many hanging draped and layered fabrics of that time. But then, and now in memory, I fingered the velvets and heavy brocade cottons. I ran my hand along the scarf fringes as I hid below a table. The fabric felt precious and silky, making me think not: "We are rich," but more: "Life is lovely."

But then my mother, that lovely creature, that lovely remote person, died. My life went skittering off in a strange direction.

I might have become a doctor even if my mother hadn't died when I was five. My father was a doctor, my grandfather, and my uncle. I came from an English and Scottish line of middle class country doctors on my father's side. Howards were doctors in India and Brazil and Australia, for they'd traveled with the British Empire. A great-aunt, Lavender Howard, in England, worked on a family tree, writing around the world to gather up information. One uncle or cousin of some kind, Doctor James Howard, had been on British ships during the Crimean War and one, Doctor Frederick Howard, with the armies of the North in the American Civil War.

The Modern Age

On my mother's side, most of the men were merchants, trading sugar and for all I know, slaves, in Antigua and India, profiting from the Empire. On both sides, women were wives and mothers, people who put on parties, and thought about fabric and gardens. I could have gone that way, I almost did. I was the first woman in our family to take up medicine.

It's true that women were starting to train as doctors just about that time under harsh and forbidding conditions. But I doubt if I would have had the drive if it weren't for Mother's death. I do believe it was that long illness and death that determined me to become a doctor. I was five years old. I stood in Mother's dim sickroom facing her dark-suited doctor across the bed and said, "I'm going to be a doctor." A roar of laughter greeted that statement, as frightening and unexpected to me as the roar from a gas-soaked fire. Now, as I remember that moment, there seemed to be many more men in the room than just my mother's doctor and my father, a wall of dark-suited men, secure in their authority. Laughter echoed around me, it recurred, it was the element I had to fight, which I never overcame, for even now, a girl who wants to be a doctor is a freak, unlikely to marry, unlovely. And of course I see now that it was funny, a sweet small being in her light voice saying such a thing. Who could predict that I would turn out to be so stubborn?

My mother's death. Those men's abrupt and harsh laughter. Those were the first things in my life that did not seem fair.

Helpless then, helpless now as my body ages. I have always been so afraid of being helpless and now after all is said and done I see that being a doctor didn't help either. I still face death uncertain and alone, as if with a bag held tight over my head and a panicky flutter in my chest.

But try to stay with the story.

Before my mother died, she was very sick for what seemed a long time. The doctor, a friend of my father's, came

The Modern Age

and sat by her bed and held her wrist and listened to her heart and then spoke in a low rumble to my father or aunt who hovered nearby, then left. I mastered the arts of self-effacement and eavesdropping. I sat on the stairs watching this doctor's whiskers wagging as he spoke so seriously and authoritatively to Aunt Susannah. Susannah used to say, "Children should be seen and not heard," and I was. A silent, watchful child, a listener. This silence has stood me well through much loneliness and being on the edge of social gatherings most of my life as a single woman. I was silent as though my life depended on it, which it did.

They tried to prevent me from going in to her, saying I would tire her, but she heard, and said, "Let her come." Did that happen many times or just once? I think she even asked for me to be brought. Once in the middle of the night, my father stood by my bed and said my name quietly as if he wanted to be able to say he'd tried and been unable to wake me. But I woke quickly. I'd already learned to be awake and alert on a moment. He carried me in to her, his jacket rough against my arms and cheek, and cold, as though he had just come in.

I took her wrist and listened to her heart and put my hand on her cold brow, smoothed back her rough, dark blonde, slightly greasy hair. She wanted me to keep doing this. She sighed and said, "Don't stop. Don't ever stop." I lost interest long before she wanted me to stop. If only I could have kept going, but my arms got tired. I was sleepy.

What comes to me now is that life-long feeling of helplessness when she died, or that she died. Why couldn't I save her? Why couldn't the calm physician with his aura of power save her? Why couldn't my father, who was also a doctor, save her? Later I grew to distrust this aura of power that I saw was part of the doctor's repertoire. Its purpose was to instill trust. And it did. But not in me. I tried to control this feeling of helplessness. At that time, disease was mysterious, capricious. Who was to be blamed? Mysterious rashes and itches would go through a whole family. Doctoring was sitting by a woman's bed, holding her hand, instilling trust, while she died mysteriously. I suppose my mother had some kind of virus. It was never explained. Or was it pneumonia? I went into obstetrics and pediatrics because it seemed more real. I remain afraid and helpless in the face of death. You'd think the introduction of sulfa drugs and other miracles during the Second War would have eased this feeling. But no. Or too late for me to appreciate. I wished to control the flash fire of illness that comes onto a body, to keep bodies alive. It's stupid. And who can control the forces that bring on war and starvation? This helpless rage is not something I wish to disclose to the Medical Society.

Then, I spent much time in my mother's bedroom under a table draped with dusty fabric. Or under the tea table in the library, trying to understand. So much time in these dusty places, listening to the grownups, that I have something, I think an allergy. I sneeze at the least sign of dust. My tables now are hard and shiny, polished wood, Danish teak, undraped. My windows have sheers only, the light pours in. The floors are bare and shiny. A woman comes twice a week and takes away the dust. Everything out in the open. Cold, I guess, as so many reactions are. I hate to think I live an unbalanced life in reaction to my childhood. I should be above that. But then why should I? No one else is. I always set such high standards for myself.

Once I sneezed and was discovered and removed from the room in Aunt Susannah's hard hands. They'd bundled Mother up and taken her out of the house. I sat quietly under the table at tea time to learn that she had gone for "electrical" treatment, absolutely the newest thing. Uncle Cornelius spoke enthusiastically about electricity. Bolts coursing through her, electrotherapy in wet clothes wound around her limbs. My stomach knotted, I felt cold at the sound of this. I panicked and sneezed. Susannah pulled me out and pushed me into the nursery, all the way down a long hallway and up the stairs. I sneezed and sneezed and sneezed.

The Modern Age

Later I found out what this was – this Faradization treatment Uncle Cornelius was so enthusiastic about. It was out of style by the time I entered training, but still on the books. "Feet are set in water connected to the negative pole of a magnetic coil. For ten to twenty minutes, electrical currents are applied to forehead, temples, top and back of head and neck, and up and down the spinal column. Visible waves of intestinal contractions ripple over the chest and abdomen. The muscles and skin of the back and lower extremities contract. Some patients end the treatment refreshed. Others are dizzy, faint, nauseous. Some will have defecated. Often there is a delayed reaction of muscle pain, nervousness, headache, insomnia. Some patients suffer minor electrical burns on their skin, pricking and burning sensations, peeling and redness of skin, pimples, or welts. If the treatment was successful, the patient bloomed." So my medical text said. I've just looked it up again. That description seems to epitomize the relish with which medical men push and prod and alter human flesh. I don't suppose in the end it will seem any more barbarous than some of the treatments we think are efficacious today. How far can we go? Now I sit here in horror, thinking: did my fragile proper mother defecate? The treatment definitely did no good.

Penny has phoned. She also wants to see me. I suspect a conspiracy. She says she has the Beatles record everyone is talking about and she wants to play it for me. "I Want to Hold Your Hand". Actually I heard it on the CBC last night. Slightly uncanny to have heard it and then have her call about it but I suppose it's just what everyone is all excited about. Morgan is officially worried. His wife is worried. They think I'm careless. It's hard to resist teasing them, to resist telling them wild stories about almost being hit by a car or robbed by a young thug. They shudder; they shake their heads. Well if this is really being written for Penny and Sarah, I had better not be harsh about their parents. I love them both dearly, Morgan and what's-her-name, and they are very kind and helpful to me. How would I be able to live on my own here in this apartment

The Modern Age

if it weren't for their help? Next time the phone rings I'll ignore it. The dog wants to walk and I must get something to feed them for tea.

I'm back. I have two hours before I have to put the kettle on. On with the story.

Before Mother got sick, I believed that the age of five was the best age in the world. Old enough to think and be free and run in the garden, and not expected to go to school or work. I remember running down the stone steps at the side of the house to the terrace where light caught in the smooth stone and where snowball flowers hung over the wall. I was allowed to pick the snowballs in big fragrant handfuls. I played as if in a secret place with stones and small sticks, making cities and people and dramas in the sandy surface of the concrete, the sun dappled through the trees hanging over the wall. Mother appeared through the French doors carrying a glass of lemonade for me and smiling. I thought I was alone and invisible, but also lovingly watched and attended. Running and feeling such joy that my feet exactly fit the stones and my legs were strong and I was fast and alive and five.

Then darkness, a long period, it must have been only weeks but it seemed long and utterly dark with sleet and slush everywhere, while my mother was sick. You have to get better; you have to take care of us, I told her, stroking her arms. Yes I will get better, she said straining, trying to sit up. But she didn't. She said I helped her when I ran my cool fingers over her hot forehead. She asked me to keep doing it. She asked me to stroke her arms and her back. But I didn't want her to turn away from me so I could stroke her back. I refused. She said I helped but she kept getting sicker and there was nothing I could do.

Her room was darkened. Before she was sick, the light streamed in and the creamy walls glowed. Her dresses shimmered. There were flowers everywhere: in tall vases and little crystal cups, flowers floating in bowls, and bushing out of huge jars. Light bounced off the beveled edges of her mirror and made rainbows dance around her room. She let me go into her scarf drawer in the curved and shining wooden dresser and pull out the long bright pieces of chiffon and silk. I danced with fabric sliding along my neck. It was heaven. She was heaven.

Before she was sick, when she knew my father was coming home late, we'd declare a holiday and I rested in her arms while she read to me and we ate cinnamon biscuits dipped in her black milky tea. Or gingersnaps. She was heaven, then she turned away from me. I was abandoned. She turned her back to me.

Her friend and sister-in-law, my Aunt Susannah, had come for a holiday all the way from England on a ship. Perhaps she meant to stay, to leave her marriage. Perhaps she meant to see if she could live in such a different place. She came to visit and stayed to nurse her friend to death. Susannah hung dark curtains on the windows to keep the light from hurting my mother's eyes. She muffled the clock and shushed me to death. She made me wear slippers instead of the heavy shoes I liked to clomp around in because they made me feel big. Perhaps I always thought Susannah brought the darkness and the illness. Perhaps that coloured my feeling towards her always.

Then Cornelius came too, Susannah's husband, my mother's brother. The Faradization was his idea. Cornelius was a big man, tall and heavy, but not fat. He had big lips, which he pursed in a humorous way. People said of him that he had a "twinkle" and indeed he did. Now though my opinion of what that "twinkle" was, or meant, has changed quite a bit. "Twinkle" is a cute word and Cornelius was not cute. I remember him at the lake in a dark wool bathing suit. White powerful legs with a filigree of dark hair on his tanned arms and neck. Throwing me up in the air and into the lake with a splash, breathless, always too much, too fast, too rough. Rough tickling.

The Modern Age

Aunt Susannah was a dull plain sort of woman; no doubt she'd been shinier in her youth before marriage to Cornelius took off her edges. Dull and smooth. She and my mother were great friends and that's probably why she married Cornelius, my mother's brother. Perhaps in a way she was really in love with my mother. It happens. She had no children and, unlike some couples who are childless and grow into each other, she and Cornelius were estranged, unlike, unlikely. Her thin hair would not stay up and she had a poor sense of fashion. She always looked like she was coming undone. The styles of the time, the close fitting dresses with trains and fullness at the back, didn't suit her. They bunched around her body where they should have stretched out. My heart aches for her with her hair pulled off her thin face. In these newer freer times she could have been something quite different. I've tried to imagine what she could have been, given more opportunities. Possibly she would have ended up in the same situation, a loveless marriage, a childless life, without resources or sense of meaning or liveliness. But what if she had discovered, oh I don't know, that she loved to look at rocks and to wander over mountains picking up bits of rock and hauling them in a dusty packsack back to camp to sit around a fire and rub her stiff and abraded hands together? I could see Susannah doing that, her hair short and flying up around her sunburned face, wearing shorts and big boots, a bit looser, a bit freer. Susannah laughing. She might have done that. She might have been happy. As it was, she tried hard, she had an inner sweetness, a refusal of bitterness, and I'm grateful to her.

Susannah and my mother, Elizabeth, were exactly the same age. Their mothers had been friends when pregnant in England, and gave birth on the same day. Susannah and Elizabeth had been friends all their lives. Cornelius, a year and a half younger, came up snotty nosed behind them. Then he went away to India and came back a man to make love to Susannah and marry her. I thought it was lazy of him to marry his sister's dear friend. He just used relationships that had been built by somebody else. I try to think that without blaming Susannah, who had limited options, no money, and a family

The Modern Age

evaporated by death and ruin. He must have been brilliant in some way because he started from nothing and became a rich man, trading in Antigua and Canada and England, moving sugar and, for all I know, slaves, around the world, making money. He was ambidextrous.

My father's father had money from the patent medicine he invented and successfully marketed. My father let his brother-in-law, Cornelius, invest for him, making much more money. This is all a mystery to me but it was fine, very fine, to have money, to be the first to have electricity, the best in plumbing, fine fabric, to be able to travel, and, I thought to send me to college. But that part of the story comes later.

Aunt Susannah was the one who told me officially that my mother had died; though I knew because I'd been there, in the room. Susannah took me on her strange bony lap. I didn't know what it meant, and I knew exactly what it meant, that my mother had died. She was going to heaven, whatever that was, and I'd see her again there in the future. Said Susannah. Maybe that accounts for my lifelong sense that something was just around the corner. For my longing. Something sweet had been offered and then snatched away, something was always missing. I was always longing for my mother's arms, that sense of shelter and acceptance, for her hectic brightness, her smile, her softness. I don't remember any of this really. Just a blur of light where she had been and three stiff photographs that did not look anything like the blur of light. I'm in about the same state of mind now, now that I'm eighty-five. I don't know what death means. I know exactly what it means. Suddenly you are just gone. I must be afraid, I think.

Now death seems close, like the roaring of a creek heard through the trees on a hike. We used to take the ferry across Burrard Inlet and climb up Hollyburn Mountain on Sunday instead of going to church. Soon I will see that rushing water. What form will it take? A fall on a nasty bit of sidewalk? A flu that won't go away? A stroke, heart attack? I'm so healthy and so close to death. Or perhaps I could live another ten years. Many live to ninety. It's not unusual these days. I read the obituaries in the newspaper every day and note mostly ages: younger than me, older, younger. The roaring of the creek through the dark trees. I will be swept away. That's all I know for sure. The trick of course is to stay awake until then. Eschew bitterness and regret. Ha ha.

My half-brother George, Morgan's grandfather, came into my life at the time of Mother's dying, summonsed from college to be there for the passing. She and I had been alone in a blissful place and I didn't realize that the sullen young man who appeared at our table at Christmas in a frock coat and cloth topped boots was connected to me. My half-brother by my father's first marriage I was told, or figured out, much later. But when my mother died he came for a longer time, and I was told that his mother had died too. We spent many hours waiting together in the library with its golden walls and large windows with many panes of milky glass. Things happened so slowly and he was kind to me and showed me pictures in books and advertisements in newspapers. We sat on a couch in the library and the fabric was rough against my bare arms and he smelled of some kind of soap and underneath scared sweat. He spent long times in his room washing and once I saw him at the washstand with morning light on the bright blue washing bowl and jug. He had his shirt off; his nipples had a tracing of dark hair around them.

Oh something's just come back to me. One day while my mother was sick, Cornelius decided we would have a family photograph done. He hired the photographer to come to the house without asking permission of anyone.

He told the maid to get my mother dressed in her finest silks. "Come on Lizzie, this won't take long. It won't hurt," he said as she came slowly into the living room with Aunt Susannah hovering behind. The photographer was quietly setting up his lights. They were electric, a novelty, very bright. This is my first conscious memory of my half-brother, George.

The Modern Age

He was pale and silent, studious and obedient. He and I and Aunt Susannah had all been instructed by Cornelius to dress in our best.

When my father came in, still carrying his black leather doctor's bag, Mother's face was pale and shiny with sweat and we were all sitting strained and silent, waiting for the photographer to be ready. We'd been sitting for an age, who knows how long? I was little; time is long. Every once in a while Susannah gave Mother a sip of water or patted her hand. I tried to come to my mother's lap but was shooed away by Cornelius. "You'll mess her." She looked at me with silent pleading eyes. "Later," I heard her promise, but perhaps only in my mind.

My father came in, looked around.

"Ah good," said Cornelius, "just in time."

Father ignored him. He saw Mother, took in her shiny face, her pallor, went to her, knelt, held her hands. "Elizabeth, what are you doing up?" She nodded at her brother Cornelius, rocking on his toes.

The photographer stood up from his bank of lights. "I'm ready."

I still have that 1885 family picture: the heavy figured drapery, the heavy dark furniture, the lace collars, the women in tight jackets and skirts with ribbons sewn around the bottom. The man, Cornelius, bald with sideburns. The mustaches and beards.

After tea I stayed quiet under the table with my view of my father's dark legs pacing and my uncle bouncing on his toes. Mother had been taken back to bed. Susannah was with her. My father paced. "What on earth could you have been thinking, getting her up for that?"

"Ah Charles, don't be so upset. It's a wonder of the new age." I looked out. Cornelius paddled his hands as though doing the breaststroke in shallow water and made his big mouth purse up. "Don't get so riled. Go easy. She's dying anyway. One little hour sitting up won't make a difference. You'll be happy to have the picture."

Now I'm shocked that he would say that so crudely. Perhaps my memory is wrong, has added something

In the photo that I hold now, my mother is the centre, seated, looking as sick as she was. If you didn't know she was sick you might think she was angry, a shrew, a mean-mouthed person. But she was holding on by a thread, concentrating. My father stands behind her, his hand on her shoulder, whiskers bristling with anger. Beside him, my uncle, twinkling, and my brother pale and fading out of the conflict. Aunt Susannah is as plain as can be, all scraped back, held back, sitting beside my mother. She's the only one not staring at the camera. I'm on a stool at my mother's knee, matching my father in fierceness, concentrating on becoming invisible. The sheen of silk in the women's clothes is offset by the darkness of the men's. The women's clothing takes up a great deal of room. There's a smell in the air of hot lights, burning fabric, sweat and anger.

The people in that photograph died one after another (as people do). My mother first, my father, my brother, Cornelius, and finally Susannah. Eighty years later I'm the only one still alive. Why does that seem so amazing to me?

And suddenly, this memory comes unbidden: "Quite the little eavesdropper aren't you?" Cornelius with his hands heavy on my shoulders. My insides upset and sharp with fear. Caught. I was under the eaves in the dripping garden peeping through a half open French door, watching him with Susannah. I was only looking for tea, hungry and dirty from a long play under the willow, and caught by a sudden rainstorm. They stood facing each other, my uncle with his head bent to see her top button, which I assume now he was trying to undo. His lips pursed. She held her face up away from his hair oil with an inscrutable look. I was trying to get a better position to see her face to try to decide what it meant when he heard me or sensed me and jumped away from her with a start.

"Mandamus," he roared, "We command." I froze. "Come in. Come here. Sit silent." He grabbed the back of my dress. I ran from his hand, slipped the collar, and hid under the shelf in the linen closet, inhaling dark starchy sheets. No-one came to find me, to care for me. I think now that my father must have thought the servants were caring for me. When I finally came out, the house was quiet. No one knew I was hiding, no one cared. Cornelius had apparently forgotten completely and gone out to a party. My father wasn't there. I kept thinking about her look, Susannah's hand at her throat when she saw me, his big red face. No one ever told me anything about men and women until I got to medical school. And what I learned from Hugo, which seemed completely different, a different subject, or men and women in a different universe entirely.

When Mother died, Cornelius tried to take me away from my father. The pattern was already in place. He and Father argued. Now I realize that he had no real power over Father except he'd invested the money and knew all about it. That's a lot I suppose. Cornelius said that I should go to London with them because Susannah would be able to take care of me. Why I wonder? Perhaps he wanted to give her a present because their relationship was so sour. Three times Cornelius did that. The first two times he lost.

I was holding Mother's hand when the life went out of her. After the long wasting painful illness, life went like a puff of wind, like air going from a balloon. All the subtle movement in her body stopped, the pale fluttery pulse in her narrow wrist, the painful flicker of her eyes, her breath. She was there, alive, and then she was gone on the in-breath.

I wanted to shake life back into her but I didn't. I put her hand down on the green silk cover and walked to get Aunt Susannah. I walked to the living room, to the library, down the long hallway to the kitchen. I knew there was no hurry. I felt myself to have great dignity and composure.

I became a little Hindoo, soon after that. My newly discovered half-brother gave me a book on religions of the world and I read about reincarnation. The experience of my mother's breath disappearing like that kept coming back to me. Where did her life go? It felt like a thing, or at least a force, a something. Did it just end? I went back to the room after the body had been removed. Someone had pulled back the long dark green damask curtains and opened the French doors to the little stone terrace. I imagine her life slipping out over the sunny stones, up over the trees. The priest talked about heaven but there didn't seem to be a container for the air, for the life that went into the air. How would it find its way if it was going to heaven? There seemed to be so much air.

TWO

I feel like I've been stuck with arrows. Morgan. His wife. I can understand them. But Penny too. They've decided to take the bull by the horns. I'm the bull. Struck by arrows, turning every which way. They want me to go into a home, A Home. A Home For Old People.

"No," I said. My voice was firm. I'm sure it was firm, but my cup rattled in its saucer. I am deeply and thoroughly panicked by this woman, Morgan's wife. Alright I can remember her name, Linda. She acts like a bossy daughter-in-law with her yellow hair, but is no relation to me. My half-niece's son's wife. What does that make her?

The Modern Age

"Auntie Em," she kept saying, with her hands out, appealing. She is unappealing to me.

"No," I say. I tried to stand, to move away from this ridiculous conversation. But it takes me so long to get up from my chair these days, pushing on the arms, that the effect was ludicrous. Morgan can't help getting up to help me, and I took his hand to steady myself. Just reflex, to take his hand. What a mess. We two are standing with my hand in his, and how I love to feel that dry skin of his. I'm lost for a moment in that feeling. But I'm angry and stubborn and it feels like time for them to go. I said, "I have to get dinner on." Linda got up. Even though they'd scarcely drunk any tea, they were off. Like bad kids, relieved to be gone.

"Just think about it," Linda said at the door. Well at least it was a short interview. Usually they sit for ages, making painstaking small talk. I prefer it when Morgan comes alone. He and I don't mind being silent together. I admit, to myself only, that I like them to come and I'm annoyed when they wait too long between visits. But now this. Usually I stand at the window and wave until they're in the Buick and gone but this time I just stood. I'm truly rattled. Could they tell?

Well I won't think about it. But then Penny. The worst of it is that Penny is on their side. I thought she was coming to tea and was disappointed when she wasn't. But she showed up later with the Beatles. First she played Love Love Me Do. And then she said, "Did they talk to you about the Home?" I won't think about it.

But Penny's on their side. That's so hard to take. She wants me put away too. Penny is funny. Twenty-seven. She still lives with her parents in the house that once was mine. She's working on her doctorate but says she doesn't have enough money to get her own place. If she gets a proper teaching position she'll move into an apartment near me she says. Or she did say. Now she wants me to go into a Home, apparently. Her sister Sarah, older by six minutes, doesn't bother with me much.

The Modern Age

Penny's thesis is in history and she is doing something on Women's Suffrage. Whatever it is requires her to go to England later this year for at least six months. I'll miss her, though I choke on sentences like that. I don't say them out loud. I will miss her though. She and I have a secret sisterhood, the sisterhood of the unmarried women. We've never spoken of this but she is funny about being a lonely gal, mugging the Paul Anka song: "I'm just a lonely boy, lonely and blue." She always brought me her music to play on my hifi and instructed me on the singers of the day. So I got to know Paul Anka and Elvis Presley, and Buddy Holly. At first she and Sarah did it together but Penny still brings me music as a grown-up, if that's what she is. She still seems awfully young to me. Penny is quiet and surprises me with hugs. She's cheerful and a bit naïve. A little bit disorganized it seems, but she works hard. It seems that when I was her age I was a lot older. How could she turn against me now?

I shall be Obdurate. Obtuse, if necessary.

A bad night. All my bones aching and no rest for the wicked, as Susannah used to say. I'm determined to continue this. I will not moan about my situation. I have this story to tell, and I will tell it. Here is the race: me, and my aging body versus this story, with their thing about me going in a Home as a distraction, a spoiler. A grey day in January, the dog has been walked, go. My mother died, then what? Go.

After my mother's death, there was a time of peace. The leaves turned colour brilliantly. This is a definite memory: my hand in my father's, light in the yellow leaves, a puff of wind and a drift of leaves. My father and I saw Susannah and Cornelius off on a ship. After a long period of cold, it was summer again. I remember little from this time, just a few vivid scenes. I was left more or less alone. No one told me what to wear or what to do or what to eat. I sometimes found clothes laid out for me by the servants and I would wear them. Dresses with flouncy skirts and fussy bits. Sometimes I went into my mother's room and put on her clothes, which were still hanging there. Midnight blue chiffon with sparkles on the bodice. I held up the skirts so I wouldn't fall on the stairs. I went out to meet my father on the step. No one said anything. Silence. Acceptance or neglect? I couldn't say.

What comes back to me now is that I knew my father was home by the smell. His feet must have been tired from going around hospitals and to people's sad houses. How he kept doing it after my mother died I don't know. He came home and took off his boots and put on slippers and the smell of male feet toasting filled the library. If I had ever managed to get and keep a husband I would have done exactly what I did with him as a child: slip into the room and rub my cheek against his cold rough face. Then stand against him, twisting his hair in my fingers.

I was neither happy nor unhappy during this time, but now believe I was scarcely alive, asleep maybe, and did not wake up again until Zoë was born. One thing that makes me shake my head with regret is that I did not come alive while my father was still there. He was gone so suddenly.

One day he stood in the front hall, holding a pile of letters, frowning. I came down the stairs quietly and slipped my hand into his, hanging by his side.

"Oh hello. How are you?"

"Why are you frowning?"

"I didn't know I was frowning."

"Well why?" I pulled his long fingers apart and bent them back. He patted my head with the letters.

"Nothing to frown about really. Cornelius is coming for

another visit."

"Uncle Cornelius?"

"Yes."

"And Aunt Susannah?"

"Yes Susannah too."

I connect that to his being gone. Soon after that he was gone.

And I remember the animals. One day at the lake house, soon after my mother died, a bird flew into the glass porch, fluttered anxiously, then hit with a thud and lay twitching on the wooden floor. From that bird I learned to calm myself down and slow my beating heart so that the animal would calm itself too. I fixed up a box for the stunned bird with grass and leaves. I went into the garden and dug worms and fed it myself. I stroked its silky brown back and stilled my breathing like a Yogi and gently fed it until I thought the wing was better and released it by the lake. My broken heart. I always believed in releasing the mended animals.

Soon I had a calling: there were other wounded animals -- a cat, a rabbit, a dog. No one said anything. No one asked me a single question about the animals, no one criticized me, no one praised me. For four years I was devoted to this work. I ordered up cages and boxes from the servants and no one objected. Sometimes now, when I can't sleep, I name each animal from that time and remember their fur, their eyes, their personality. Jim the sheep dog, fun-loving, emotional, responsive, attached, who came and put his paw in my lap when Cornelius and my father argued as if to say, "Make them stop". Marion the mottled cat, aloof, demanding. She had a lump on her face which I bathed and cleaned until it popped and drained all over my hand. Marmalade and Strawberry who came together and left together. Geoffrey, the muscle dog, all male doggy energy, briefly, until he bit one of the servant's children and was taken from me. Sparrow, Rabbit, Blue Rabbit, Rabbit Family, and Robin. The hello-goodbye cats in the spring.

I believe that the animals were attracted by my great sincerity, that quality which later got me into so much trouble. With each animal there was a moment when our trust clicked or slotted into place, a moment when my stillness and openness allowed the animal to put its trust in me totally. With dogs, this was easy. They were willing to do it all the time; they did it as if their lives depended on it, which they did. But with the cats and rabbits it was harder, it took great concentration, great stillness. The birds were hardest. But there was always that moment. Sometimes they looked at me. Sometimes there was that eye to eye contact. Sometimes they simply became very still, very relaxed, surrendered. Later I criticized myself and thought I had exercised undue power over these animals as I worked to heal them.

At the time I was a serious six-year-old Hindoo and felt that I had been animal not long before, and probably would be again. I didn't believe in killing insects and I let spiders crawl over my hands as I turned them over and over. I tried to brush away mosquitoes, spiders and ants without hurting them. I would not eat meat.

All this intensity I later transferred completely to Zoë and I used some of the same skills with my patients later, much later.

I say I was a Hindoo and now I'm not sure what I meant by that. I have tried to think, but cannot remember, what book my brother gave me about religions but it must have been a picture book because I still have images of many-armed Goddesses with deep red dresses. Durga or Kali riding a tiger. Colour: the saffron of Agni or fire, black Krishna who was exchanged at birth with a girl and protected by a five-headed snake. I went just now to the lovely soft pages of the Encyclopaedia Britannica, 1911, thinking I would understand better what I meant by being a Hindoo but the article there was all dry condescension about India and Indians and the caste system. I have never read the Upanishads, and have a shallow understanding, that of a child, just a picture book knowledge, but surely there is more to it than just the caste system. Hinduism is 8,500 years old, resilient, peace-loving. And at the core is the belief that there is one divine substance pervading all.

But I think what attracted me most when I was a serious lonely girl was the idea of reincarnation, the idea that we don't really die. At some deep level I wished beings not to die, which means I was actually the most skeptical Hindoo or Christian (as I became after my father died), because I must not really have believed in reincarnation, or life after death, or whatever the words were to describe our fear of not being alive. Confused about it I suppose, and aching to know, to really know. Now I see I don't know, I won't know. I don't care for growing old. I see that inside I do not age – some part of me is green and young and unsure and yet also as cocky as ever as the body dries up and slows. I am not resigned to this. And I certainly wasn't resigned when I faced so much resistance to becoming a doctor and bullied my way through it. Well I'm not there yet in the story.

And I realize by speaking of my handling of the animals in this way, and my later patients in the same breath, I may offend, but as I said at the beginning, I don't care much anymore. I believe I have become known in the neighbourhood as a queer old duck.

When my mother died, Susannah and Cornelius wanted to take me back to England with them but my father refused. Then they came back a year or so later and tried again. But he apparently wanted me near him, even though I think I hardly ever saw him. I read a great deal. I have vivid memories of being in the library of that large house and working my way through the weird assortment of books: medical texts with early photographs of grotesque diseases, gardening books, theology, and many books of half-baked poetry, which as a six-year-old I loved. My half brother George was often in the library with me, showing me things, talking, but he lived somewhere else and came and went. He sometimes took me out ice skating on the river or to the farmers' market at Jacques Cartier Square. On market day there was snow, with horses hot under blankets, the horse smell in puffs on the cold air, wagons on runners backed into market, the wares down the middle. Men in dark coats with felt or fur hats walked around stamping and breathing. Icicles.

This just came back to me: under gas lighting my brother in a bank. It must have been the Bank of Montreal West End branch. He sat in a metal teller's cage with wood half way up the side with curled metal around his head. George in the cage was just one of many men in dark suits with large moustaches. One with high boots, ties, high collars. He sat under stone arched windows, round turrets, and peaked windows on top. I don't remember who took me to visit him there. I'm puzzled because I know he trained as a doctor and yet he was obviously not working as a doctor. He was stiff and distant in his cage. But my brother at home in the library was flesh and fun and the source of interesting facts. I liked him. And I loved his gay and beautiful fiancé, Kate, who began appearing sometime during that time. I don't understand this thing about him being a doctor. I believe he was, but from this memory he obviously worked in a bank. I'm sorry that I have no way to sort this out, no one to ask.

My father was a doctor. He took me with him sometimes on his visits. There were these memories: a flood on Rue St. Antoine with men on a raft poling through the water. Then, four men in boats with bowler hats. Tall columns outside a store emerging from water. Bright reflections. Big chunks of ice breaking up on the river. Men shoveling dark against white. Chunks of ice and snow blown up in ridges. Men standing on a

The Modern Age

hill of ice chunks. "Le debacle Le debacle," I chanted. This is almost the only French I still know.

In a house of some friends, big padded and frilled chairs everywhere. I sat on a big carpet with flowers caught in squares and played toss the beads. Chinaware on every surface. The sideboard was covered with vases, a faded screen in a corner, a large painting of a man hugging a child, candelabra on the mantel with candles burning noisily, and knick-knacks everywhere. My father was there, god-like to these patients, dispensing hope in small brown bottles.

My father didn't speak French and I think most of his patients were English or Jewish but sometimes he went into a home and he didn't speak their language. They told him the symptoms and history of the disease and he sat by the patient taking their pulse nodding. Then he'd give them some medicine, and they would nod and not understand. Sometimes one of the family would translate. Later in the carriage he would smoke.

And the year before he died, it must have been 1889, my father took me out to see the new toboggan run built up on the side of the mountain. I close my eyes to today's bright day outside and can see this: men with toques and moustaches careen down the icy chute, tipping out, laughing. A Mount Royal woman slides with dainty feet tucked in, in a long coat, laughing, with a man pressed up close behind her. Two women in fringed scarves lounge on toboggans at the bottom while two men stand with legs spread and one foot each up on the toboggan, impressing each other, flirting. So vivid. Here and now the dog barks sharply once and I am back. He barks at the birds against the window and I am here, but back then Father and I climbed long stairs up the side of the hill and then we too flew down on a borrowed toboggan, laughing.

Sometimes just before I go to sleep now I see snow on the crotch of a dark tree in a graceful white patch. That seems to be an image from that time.

The dog pushes against me to go out, but I am still back there. One of my earliest memories, but it must have been before my mother died, was of an ice palace, a gleam of square bricks of ice, lit from inside with a flag on top, a Union Jack.

When I was six or seven, I received a gift from England, from some unknown aunts: deep green velvet pants to the knees, boy's pants with white stockings. I loved them. It must have been a mistake. Susannah was there and tried to take them away from me, offering a wicker sewing basket in exchange. I wouldn't give them up and wore the pants secretly when she was there and openly when she was not.

Now I'm sitting in my upper apartment with trees shining through my windows and sunlight on red poinsettia leaves, and memories return to me as dreams return in the middle of a busy day. There was a flood. My father took me right into the worst of it. I don't remember how we got there, how we got to be looking on this without getting wet. There were men in a boat rowing through the street. La Rue something. The name is gone.

So I remember two opposite things: that he was distant and seldom around, and that I went with him to see patients and he argued for me to stay with him. I suppose both are true? All the winter scenes are bright and sparkly with men in dark coats against the snow. We weren't universally adored in those upstairs apartments with the metal balconies. We weren't always welcomed. Sometimes I was given something orange to drink. Often I stayed in the carriage. He took me to see ice hanging from a building that had burned and been sprayed by firemen, a charred ice palace. He took me on a long drive out on the river where they'd made a road in the snow with trees planted weirdly as guide posts. These beautiful adventures with my father sparkle and shine in my memory but he was distant, tall, sleepy, deeply sad, and busy. I was alone.

I have eschewed self-pity, have eschewed it all my life in perhaps too harsh a manner, but one has to look at this little girl and say she was too much alone. But perhaps not. Harsh it may be, but the self-reliance I learned is what I still need to live this unusual life. Spinster. After my mother died I lived like a little ghost for four and a half years. Spinster child.

My father's death when I was ten was very unlike my mother's. My mother died in the heart of the house, in my hands. My father just disappeared. As a medical man, looking back, I would have to say it must have been heart; there was no sign beforehand. As a woman I would say broken heart. It took five years for his heart to stop, but he never recovered from my mother's death and who knows about the mysterious wife, my brother's mother, before that.

He just seemed to be gone for a longer than usual time. I can't remember being told he was dead. I'm not sure about this. Wouldn't I have some memory of it? But it doesn't come. I can remember the dark church, the Church of England minister droning. The words: "that ye may have eternal life". So that at ten I gave up being a Hindoo and became a Christian. "That ye may have eternal life," I chanted. And I was as fanatical a Christian as could be, given my limited Church of England resources. I gave up my work with animals from one day to the next.

The minister came into our house and made some comment to my brother's new wife Kate about the dogs, the doggy smell, or the doggy footprints. I gave up the dogs and my whole work with animals and I took up Christianity. And Kate. I took up Kate as my vocation, my adoration. The minister had a round smooth face with too small for him gold glasses and a wide forehead out of which dark hair sprung. He spoke in his lovely deep voice about rebirth, how the roses

The Modern Age

returning each spring were signs. He addressed George, but Kate was there too, distracted, and I was listening intently.

Our one old dog, Jim, lived for many years after I stopped being interested but he was never sure what my attitude would be and became wary of me. I'm not saying I ever hurt him. I was just hardened to his needs. I knew that dogs would not be entering the Kingdom of Heaven and I wanted to concentrate myself in the right direction. I believe he had a happy time with the servants who were kind and amused by him. He was a sheep dog. I wish I could be with him now. The image of the servant with a dirty apron must be from this time.

I've been sitting here by the window for almost two hours between that last bit and this. Time goes. Traffic passes. The light changes. I look at my watch and think it has broken, the hands fly too fast, but all the outside clocks, the radio, the clock in the library building across the street, they all tell me I'm wrong and that I do spend two hours at a time just dreaming, the dog dozing, having given up on me. Why do I want to write this? If they could only catch and bottle those aged dreams, the shake head regrets, the smiles of remembering. Remember, remember? But it's gossamer, spider webs, broken before you even know they are there. Zoë, brightness, a theological proof that it is better to be alive than dead. I haven't got to Zoë yet and she is why I am writing. I just meander.

The darkness gathers. What is that line? My father died. At the reception there were many women, one with strong cologne, one with a red face, one pale. They said, "Your father...your grandfather..." There was fruitcake, ginger cookies, sherry, tea. I tasted everything then threw up in the downstairs bathroom. Susannah brought me a cup of milky tea and took me away. Yes, Susannah and Cornelius were there again. Why? They couldn't have come just for the funeral because there weren't airplanes.

Abide with me. Cornelius was there, holding my hand too tight. Fast falls the eventide. Susannah snuffling. It seems to me we choose to remember certain scenes, that is, choose at the time to store them in a vivid way to be remembered later. Some kind of heightened consciousness is in effect. In the dark wood of the church, I'm ten in a dark wool dress. My dress is scratchy. I have to go to the bathroom. The darkness gathers. Lord with me abide.

I threw up because Cornelius held my hand too tight. Cornelius and my brother were arguing. "I'm her godfather," said Cornelius in that deep voice. Commanding. How did my brother win? He won that time. Kate was there, pregnant, my brother's wife. I was leaning my head on her stomach. I could feel a fluttering against my cheek: Zoë. It was Kate's family that intervened. They had power (money) and they said I should stay with my brother. I heard them but I have no memory of who they were. They kept me. Later they (other ones, but still Kate's people) took Morgan away. I do not understand how this can have happened.

When I was nine, there was a flurry of excitement as this young man, my brother, became all man by marrying Kate and soon after that my father died, then Zoë was born. He didn't die like my mother in slowly gasping stages. He was there, reading the newspaper, going out, coming home, brushing my cheek with his moustache and then he was gone. I guess I was told he had died but no one ever proved it to me. He was just gone and it was like the leaves are gone from the trees, they've been raked up and burned in a pleasant fire at he bottom of the garden and will come again next year. He never came again but it was so exciting that George and Kate and then Zoë moved into my house to stay. I became a ward of my Uncle Cornelius in England but I did not realize that at the time. I was so enchanted by the baby.

When my father died, my whole life changed. I had been free for four and a half years - lonely, eccentric, but free. When my father died I became the property of my Aunt Kate. I took up Kate and then Zoë.

I said that I gave up my interest in animals because I became a Christian but I also could see that rabbits and mice and birds frightened and disgusted Aunt Kate and I wanted very much to please her, at least at first. She didn't care that I was a Christian but she was pleased that I had finally taken an interest in clothes. I'm still a bit puzzled by this connection between Christianity and nice clothes; as a Hindoo I never cared, except to drag around in my mother's things. She instructed me on the correct way to wear clothes: the importance of gloves, how to wear a hat, the right times to wear white shoes. She brought in a dressmaker who made me stand still for long excruciating periods while she stuck pins around my body. Pregnant Kate would laugh when I said, "Sit where I can see you." She had blonde hair and quicksilver skin. I wiggled until she moved into my line of sight, the dressmaker silently pressing my body in the right direction until I was still.

What my brother's wife Kate taught me was that people are not to be counted on.

I suppose I'd already learned that lesson when my mother died. But I felt most bitterly towards Kate when she turned me away. I lay in wait for her and when I heard her come from her room in the morning, I skipped into step beside her. Some mornings she was gay and took my hand and took me with her shopping or visiting and once bought me hot chocolate in a hotel dining room. Some days she did not come out of her room. And some days she came out and paced the house noisily, screeching sometimes, pushing me ahead of her, or away.

Later as a medical student I got in the habit of daydreaming about my family trying to diagnose that from which they suffered and died. I wondered about Aunt Kate, but did not have enough information, whether she was actually mentally ill. She had a sister who was locked away. I learned this from one of Kate's brothers long after Zoë died and still wonder whether I should tell Morgan and the grandnieces, but I can't think how the information could be helpful to them. Anyway the thing that Kate most suffered from was alcohol.

I'm tired now. I have to stop. I'm going out to get a locksmith to get the locks changed. Morgan is coming to tea again tomorrow to "talk to me". Stupid, hysterical perhaps to change the locks. But he does have a key and I don't ever want to be taken by surprise.

Morgan cancelled, not coming today. Stupid to feel disappointed, but now I have this little space. So to continue.

When Zoë was born, I had given up being a Hindoo, but I still believed (and in a way do so now) that Zoë was my mother reincarnated, my mother's spirit in another's body. I was going to say it could be genetics, but Zoë was not genetically related to my mother. Her grandmother was my half-brother's mother, long dead.

When I became a Christian, I went to Sunday School at the Anglican Church where my father's funeral had been. A sour-faced woman in a lilac dress led the children from the nave through a series of tunnel-like hallways to a basement room where we were instructed in Christian mysteries. Miss…can't remember her name but I can see her person quite clearly in my mind's eye. I didn't know anything about poverty at the time and was judgmental about her always wearing the same dress. I was aloof and judgmental about the other children. What a sorry friendless little person I was. I didn't believe they – children or teacher - really understood the issues. Resurrection for example. Neither teacher nor children understood what a profound gift had been given them by the life of Jesus, by his death and resurrection, by his dying for their sins. So I thought at the time. At the time it made perfect sense to me. And I also saw that this was all a metaphor, that the rebirth every spring, daffodils pulsing and tulips throbbing, this bright vegetative rebirth, was quite possibly the only resurrection we would see.

I once had a patient who had come from South America and she told me that when she first came to Canada, in winter, she wondered why we had all these dead trees around. Then they bloomed.

As a Christian, I sang little Christian hymns to Zoë in her crib and told her Christian stories about a sweet and gentle Jesus. For one Christmas, I became Mary, mother of God, and rocked my sweet baby Zoë in a manger. One night my brother stopped me from taking Zoë out into the cold to enact a manger scene in the garden shed.

I told Kate what I needed to be got up as a Christian and took myself off to Sunday School on my own, dressed up in heavy wool, hatted, and with hair curled. Alone and serious, breathing my walking prayers on the cold Montreal air. Sometimes my brother accompanied me smiling in his amused skeptical way. I suppose he thought I was cute in the way I was determined to set out on a Sunday morning with or without him. I grilled him on what he could remember of my baptism. I wished that I had not been baptized so that I could do it again and do it right. I didn't know then that there were churches where they plunged your whole body in the water or perhaps I would have stayed Christian longer and found one of those dramatic places. By the time I did find out, I'd lost my taste for submersion. I wanted to be taken as a confirmation candidate but they said I was too young. It was a quick, intense and very serious Christian immersion. The Hindooism went deeper and lasted longer. I guess I'm still more Hindoo than Christian. But no nothing, nothing at all. It doesn't matter.

And Zoë, Zoë arrived just totally herself. Of course all

babies do, as I learned, but with her it was so evident she was herself from the beginning, from her birth. She slipped out easily with her eyes open, looking around with dark unfazed eyes.

I suppose my eyes looking back at her were dark and unfazed. I think I was the first person she saw when she was born. Certainly I was the first one who actually looked back at her. Kate was beside herself. It had been a long noisy labour with a great deal of pain. I had stayed on a chair outside the room for most of it, sometimes lying down on the hall runner to rest, always ready. I went into the room on my hands and knees so the attendant women couldn't see me and was there just as the head was crowning. At first I didn't know what it was, that dark pushing between her legs. Then I did know. And then a few more pushes and Zoë!

I learned later that every birth is different. I delivered hundreds of babies over the years. I attended labours that lasted a few minutes and ones that lasted seventy-five hours. I saw laughter and tears of course. I saw babies come out quiet, grey and limp, purple and screaming, pink and well. I pulled out babies with the cord wrapped two times around their neck, with their arms up over their heads, tearing the poor mother. Births and deaths at the same time. Well so it goes, every birth with its own drama, its own rhythm. Through it all has run this amazement, the sense that life has great power, to which we must bow down. That was there at the birth of Zoë. I felt it then.

I knew what was happening, that a baby was being born. I thought this birth might be the opposite of my mother's death, like a balloon quietly being filled with air. But it was nothing like that at all. The baby, that was Zoë, came out already full up with life, inflated inside I assumed. There were several women in the room and one important looking man who had driven me out of the room several times. One of the women noticed me crouching down by the doorway of the bedroom so I could see around the women and between Kate's legs where the insistent head emerged. She nodded and held out the baby for me to see, glowing and slippery with blood, breathing already, no need for a spanking. Eyes open.

I held Zoë when she was only a few minutes old, cleaned and wrapped, self-possessed. They called me "p'tit mamam" and I was. The little mother in me rose up to meet this child, was born with her. As she grew, I spent hours with her, creating an enclosed world as my mother had done for me, singing, picking up the blocks she threw, reading to her. She was responsive always. Joyful and mischievous.

Kate was happy to have me look after her baby. Now when I look back on it, I see she had a drinking problem, as her mother and father had. I have some compassion for her now. Then, I was all judgment. She was gay in the evenings, calling us to her and showering us with kisses and endearments, grouchy in the mornings, pushing Zoë and me away and sometimes wrinkling her nose and narrowing her eyes in a menacing way. In that time and place, everyone always had a drink before dinner, but she must have had several. I've seen many drunks since then. At the time, we just learned to be careful around her. Tiptoes. But it was a big house and there were many servants to shelter us. It was easy to build a sheltered world for Zoë and me. I took Zoë out on the same light-filled terrace where I'd played happily before my mother died. I'd pick the snowball flowers and throw them to her and Zoë would laugh.

We were alone mostly, in a child's kingdom, cared for dispassionately by a succession of efficient servants, some with gentle hands when they combed our hair and some rougher and even quite mean. It didn't matter. They didn't matter. Mostly they spoke French and we spoke English because this was in Montreal and we were the ruling class and were oblivious to the people who served us.

Little Mother my brother called me, picking up the

Quebecoise teasing. He was affectionate and kind but often gone, as men are. He had a job in the bank but later I realized the money to keep the whole show going came from the herbal remedy, the cough syrup my grandfather invented and patented, and the investments Uncle Cornelius made with that money. Now I can't remember why that made me so angry as a young woman and I regret what I did with that patent medicine recipe in my anger.

My brother was in love with his wife Kate, uxorious, and gay with her in the evenings. They dressed up and went out glittering into the snow, wearing furs and carrying muffs. They laughed and shone with anticipation of a party, a dance, a dinner. They were fun, Edwardians in the New World, before Edward even came to the throne. Their gaiety was contagious, her perfume on the air. Zoë and I got excited watching them get ready to go out and, after they left, we tore all over the house up the two long staircases and down the halls to the back, into their room, still rich with perfume, to jump on their bed, laughing wildly, until some servant called us to a halt and fed us supper in the kitchen and we fell into bed tired and alone and sad.

I was not expected to go to school. Sometimes a lady in a dark skirt and white blouse came in and did arithmetic, music and Latin with me. Sometimes we were dressed up in frilly dresses and taken to a party with other children, which was agony for me, though Zoë seemed to like it. I once ripped her dress trying to get her to come away from a group of children she was playing with. Aunt Kate was angry and smacked my upper arm hard enough to leave a hand print. Then she was sorry and hugged me. I called her Aunt Kate, though she was my half sister-in-law.

Aunt Kate, eyes red-rimmed, hair flying in straw bunches, bearing down on me, screaming, "Mary-Margaret, how dare you?" What had I done? I don't remember. Something like: left a towel on the floor or put a dirty handprint on the wallpaper. She taught me to lie, reflexively, automatically. To wail: "I didn't didn't. Maid did it."

And Aunt Kate, hair smooth and silky, standing behind me, gentle hand on my shoulder, looking at ourselves in the mirror, "So pretty, so pretty," she murmurs and tucks a piece of hair back from my face.

After Zoë was born, I became a different person. I didn't have to live in books and stories and with animals. I mothered her until she was big enough to play and then I played with her. I went backwards. Instead of being wise and sad and big-eyed and lonely, I became a child, but still a peculiar child. Zoë filled up the world for me.

I'm trying to figure out how to write about Zoë. How to describe her? There's this sort of coloured blur in my memory. The blur is singing in Quebecois French, laughing, moving. She's twirling, or bent over in a back bend. Why should I have to remember Zoë? Why write about her? She is drawing, colouring, painting, her fingers hardly big enough to hold the crayons. Intent on her project.

Zoë, because so much of what I did had to do with her. And so much of what I didn't do had to do with her death. Now there are so many things I wish I'd done differently. It makes this business very difficult to write, perhaps impossible. I notice I've wandered right off the project of writing about becoming a lady doctor. I wake up in the night with a memory and shaking my head as though to shake it off, shake it into a different world, a world in which I would have acted properly and done it properly and all would be different. Regrets I suppose. When people say they have no regrets, they mean they are unrepentant and I am not that. Do you think if I had acted differently Zoë would still be alive? A brief fantasy: Zoë and I almost the same age as we get older, the ten years making less and less difference, supporting each other down the street with our shopping bags over our outside arms.

But I don't want to make it sound like some kind of Boston friendship, or that I was secretly in love with her. Maybe. I suppose I have to consider that. But I did love men, well one man in particular, Hugo, but I don't think that's relevant. Zoë was special and what I felt for her was special. Not exactly motherly because we were orphans together. Sisterly maybe, but I've seen lots of sisters who are distant and careless about each other, meeting only with cold kisses at Christmas and family weddings. Zoë was my niece, my friend, my daughter, my dear dear Zoë. The air is filled with "if only" as evening falls.

She would never be my companion in this old age business anyway. She wouldn't really grow old like me and she would not be so lonely. She was fertile and her son and granddaughters are kind and attentive to me but they would be close and passionately attached to her. They say they are coming again to talk to me, all of them at once. I refuse to be nervous. Stay with the hypothetical aged and lovely Zoë, face glowing with aliveness and love, a coloured blur where now there is nothing.

A night has passed, refusing to be nervous. Another day, sitting and muttering. Have I been clear? I can't bear to read what I've written and think I've left something out. Or repeated myself. Round we go again. This is what it's like to be old. Did I say that at my father's funeral I became a Christian for a time when the solemn priest intoned the words about how Jesus died and rose from the dead so that we may see that life is eternal? I can't remember the actual words. I was ten and my dress itched. If Jesus died, and then was alive, then we all might be alive after death. If Jesus could come alive, then my father could, my brother the rosy-cheeked guardian and friend of the book, even my dear mother. Except for this problem, noticed in obituaries which I read during this time: the obituary says he has gone to be reunited with his beloved wife but he was married twice, with which wife will he be reunited? Of

The Modern Age

course this is childish. But now I feel that the consolation of Christianity is childish. I went to church the other day for the funeral of an old friend. It seemed infantile, the consolation of promised resurrection like a sweet cookie when you've stubbed your toe. It can't be like that. But still, if Jesus died and then was alive, I may yet find Zoë and explain to her. But I don't, I really don't believe that now. Don't ask me what I do believe.

Zoë's age was the Modern Age. If the age had been allowed to come to adulthood, if it had not been cut off by that savage regression, The War. What a stupid daydream I have, an age of smooth enlightenment in which Zoë never died, my lover returned, I had many children, and the War never happened. The Wars. The First World War, the Second. What next? Nostalgia for a Golden Age that never got properly born. Stupid.

The other thing: I may have given the wrong impression about the servants. I said we were distant and ignored them? Something like that. That was me who did that, not Zoë. What I woke up with this morning was the realization, or remembrance, that Zoë spoke French. I'd totally forgotten until I sat in the window for about an hour this morning, that feeling of terrible exclusion when Zoë at three or four ruled the kitchen, with its white enamel countertops and kitchen cross with Jesus bleeding. She kneeled up on a chair, chattering with two or three dark-haired thin people, who I scarcely could distinguish, in a language I did not understand.

Zoë at three was self-possessed. The women in the kitchen loved her. They were from St. Jovite, a village north of the city. We went there once with them, to their small homes, a place of snow, small maple trees, and cracking lakes north of the city. The kitchen was the warmest room in the house. I see now that I have exaggerated this sense of being alone. Now I must try not to sentimentalize these people, these noble peasants. Just be aware they existed. They brought us maple syrup from those trees. They lived in a world that was real to them. But not to me.

      Also I see now that I felt I owned Zoë. I wanted to hold her tight like a precious thing, my precious exclusive thing. Cover her with a cloth when I couldn't be around like a parrot in a cage. Obviously she had her own life. No one could own her. That made me so angry. I can feel my stomach tightening with it now. But Zoë was what we call a "charmer". My rage dissolved when she turned to me. I lay awake last night or this morning, after I realized she spoke French as a child, and a whole scene came back to me. The kitchen is dim and closed for the night. We are supposed to be in bed asleep, but we are roaming the house and have come to the dark kitchen. We slide open the tin bread drawer, put our hands into the fresh bread and scoop it out, eating the yeasty white bread as we run, bursting with suppressed laughter.

THREE

Penny is gone. How could I have misunderstood everything so completely? I truly must be losing my marbles. I thought she wasn't going for several months. But she's gone now. Gone to London to research her thesis. She's going to stay in the Holland Street house, which came to Morgan when Susannah died and has been let all these years. Morgan was here again last night. He brought a casserole from Linda. He didn't mention moving me but kept eyeing me as though speculating on what it would take. Or perhaps I'm getting too suspicious as well as senile. What a blow to lose Penny like that. She says that she'll write. I feel like going back to bed and pulling the covers over my head, but something pulls me on, seats me at this desk, this typewriter, and so, pressing down the

The Modern Age

lonely place she leaves and the anxiety about what Morgan wants, to take a deep breath and to continue.

In 1895, when I was fifteen, I went to live for a year in London with Aunt Susannah and Uncle Cornelius.

The first impression after the long trip was a big house, a cold night, a fire, men clustered around the fire, waiting for women to come to close the circle to light up the night, to provide the warmth. Drinks before dinner in the living room, then sitting around a large table lulled by merry talk. Who were all those men? There always seemed to be lots of people around. I was introduced and can't remember who they were at all. I believe my future lover Hugo was there that first night.

During my first few days I went slowly around the house, looking at and running my hands over smooth and shiny exotic things gathered from Empire: brass rail in front of the hearth and brass wood basket, fringed floral pillow, silver tea pot with tall curved handle, tall vase on the mantle holding one dried rose, box wrapped in a shiny scarf pulled up and fastened at the top, shiny blue tiles across the top of fireplace, stained glass crest in the window. It was all strange, strangely beautiful, and heavily ugly at the same time.

I was in London to be "finished", a vague process to which I was deeply resistant but which was insisted on by Kate and Aunt Susannah. Much later it occurred to me that Cornelius was as much behind the idea as anyone. Sometimes he made comments about people's class like, "They're not landed gentry. They're solidly middle class. As we are. We're not ashamed of it and you can be properly finished, Young Lady." We were wealthy, but as traders, and he had pretensions.

My body had rushed ahead of me and become womanly. Kate had made sure I had what I needed: the dresses to come into dinner, the ability to put my hair up, the gloves.

The Modern Age

But I felt a child still, awkward and out of sorts. I was lonely and missed Zoë terribly at first, though I am ashamed to say that after I met Hugo I didn't think about her from moment to moment, or even sometimes day to day.

It was summer in London; the streets smelled of lime trees, that mysterious sweetness which I couldn't place until I finally asked Susannah and she pointed up into the glossy green leaves. I could see the small creamy blossoms and wondered that such a big emanation came from such a small bloom.

Aunt Susannah was in the middle of some kind of brittle and bitter awakening, which took the form of athletic verbal jousting with Cornelius each night after dinner. It made me uncomfortable and frightened. Surely women had been murdered for less. She was very bold with him. She was a member of a Women's Suffrage Society. Two years before, New Zealand had given women the right to vote. Susannah was electrified by this. "Why not England?" she would ask querulously. Over the years, Susannah traversed the whole spectrum of political involvement: starting with the relatively mild National Union of Women's Suffrage Societies, standing back and debating the crazy radicalism of the Women's Social and Political Union led by Emmeline Pankhurst, joining in, even volunteering to be arrested though not being accepted. Finally, she stopped all her political activity and would just shake her head tight-lipped if the subject came up. Women's voting rights would not come to England or Canada until after the First War. But when I was there in 1895, her intellectual explorations and this battle became the principal events of the days. She spent hours at her small desk, a bent comic figure writing impassioned letters. Her time with me was spent in lectures, interspersed with rigid tea visits and polite or boisterous dinners with Susannah guiding me with her hard bony hand.

The living room or parlour where all these dramas, this to-ing and fro-ing took place was upstairs in their house in

The Modern Age

Holland Street near Sloane Square. The room was large but filled up with fabric and furniture so that it seemed small again. Small tables scattered throughout the room were hung with lace or velvet or striped cotton cloth. Each cloth was fringed, each fringe frayed. The colours were dark: burgundy and mahogany; the windows large, but swathed in fabric, and the glass dim.

Susannah was not an avid housekeeper. Several dogs slept by the fire or, when no-one was about, on the couches, so the room was dusty and there was a light layer of golden dog hair everywhere, especially on the deep burgundy figured carpet in front of the big fireplace. You didn't notice in the fire lit evening when everything glowed slightly.

Cornelius loved the dogs. He pulled their ears and talked baby talk to them, pursing his mouth and bending his big body over them. They really only roused themselves when he came in the room. I could get them up and playing by showing a ball and promising a romp in the garden, but they only loved Cornelius. Susannah politely and pointedly ignored them.

That family was prodigious with fires. One burned all day and long into the night so the room was always pleasantly warm and well lit by the standards of the day. Theirs was one of the first homes to get electric lights and these proved to be dimmer than the gas lights which preceded them.

There were no books in the room but many popular magazines which both Cornelius and Susannah read with avid attention. They subscribed to Punch and The Academy and several others and would often read each other bits from one or the other of them, whooping or cackling with laughter, or shaking their heads in disbelief. This gave me a different sense of their marriage than I had when I was little and saw them in Canada. The magazines piled up on the many tables until one day Susannah bundled them all up and took them to the kitchen demanding that the seservants do something with them. I think the servants enjoyed this very much.

One morning soon after I arrived, Aunt Susannah came into the dining room with something in her hand. It was a photograph in a silver frame of three women with sashes across their chests. One of them was my mother. She'd also been a suffragette of sorts it seemed; at least she'd gone to a few meetings and daringly stood on street corners handing out pamphlets before my father whisked her off to a new life in the colonies. Susannah was cross with herself for being so timid in those days and, though she still didn't march or pamphleteer, she was determined to try to persuade Cornelius of the rightness of the position. I thought, and still think, that was a waste of time. Trying to persuade him I mean.

The women who worked to get the vote were revolutionaries. They led lives in which the consequences of their actions were not known and took actions that their fathers and brothers and husbands believed were crazy. These men believed that, of course women should have the vote, but their daughter, sister, or wife should not die for it, throwing herself in front of a horse or starving to death in a civilized British jail. I personally love change. I love an upset apple cart but I also love my comforts, my safety, my home. Would I truly go off the deep end? Now it seems self-evident: of course women have the vote (except in Switzerland of course). Of course of course. It was self-evident then but still not at all clear that we would win. So I too became a suffragette at the age of 15 in London in 1895. Now I wished that I had marched and handed out pamphlets, but I was timid too and Susannah, for all her wild talk, too proper. But it was stirring and exciting and we sneered at the men who did not wholly support us.

Cornelius said, "Of course women should have the vote, but do you really think Molly Jones is ready to take on such a high degree of citizenship? You my dear, if it was you, I would trust you to choose the cabinet if it came to that, but I have my doubts about Molly Jones."

Molly Jones was his way of saying working class,

women below our station, though I'm sure he had no idea whether Molly Jones knew anything about politics or not and in his heart of hearts was sure that she would vote against his interest and towards her own. That seems so obvious now, but I'm amazed how much hard mental work it's taken me to see that.

"My dear Susannah, you are quite misguided," said Cornelius, standing at the fireplace violently moving about the figurines. Cornelius had big meaty hands and small feet. His stomach was carried to the front but he was not fat. His broad forehead was quite red and dark against the thick white hair swept back from his face. "And you would agree surely that it is natural and right for a woman to be a mother."

"Yes of course, but…"

Over-riding her, "Then I say to you that when a woman persists in this individualism, and demands equal rights and whatnot, she denies her own natural function and will destroy her own spiritual development and eventually the whole race."

This was cruel because Susannah had been unable to have children and carried a huge sadness about this. For once, she was unable to bring herself to answer Cornelius and you could tell that she wondered if her own spiritual development had been twisted by her infertility, and perhaps whether her interest in advancing the cause of women had somehow caused her childlessness. She had terrible pain each month. I now suppose it was fibroids but I think she never saw a doctor. She was silent. I was silent but almost bursting with outrage on my prickly chair.

Later she plumped down beside me on the red couch, "There's a woman pirate in the South China Sea with a thousand ships at her command and I have to beg to vote. Hmmph."

"You'd go about in bloomers and make speeches like some Florence Nightingale?"

"No I'd spend my time collecting beetles and reptiles for the British Museum."

"But you could do that now, couldn't you?"

A grimace.

Susannah told me wonderful stories about women she'd heard of who did strange things, masqueraded as men, were bold and courageous. I have no idea whether she made them up, embellished them, or whether any of them had even a grain of truth. She told me about a woman who dressed up as a man and took a job as a stage coach driver, how women dressed as men in the American Civil War. "Sarah Edmonds from Canada was one," she said.

One night Cornelius came out of the blue with, "Women undertaking serious study are ruining their health." I'd said nothing about my secret determination to be a doctor and flushed guiltily as if I'd been caught.

In those days, women couldn't learn Latin or Greek unless they had private tutors and you couldn't go to medical school without Latin or Greek. It was better in Scotland Susannah told me. There a woman could actually be educated. After this challenge from Cornelius, Susannah decided to be subversive and hired me a tutor. Another woman in a white blouse and dark skirt, like the one back in Canada, but more sophisticated, came to the house with a satchel full of books. Susannah did it out in the open so that Cornelius wouldn't pay any attention. She decided to learn too. She and I studied together for a while. Greek, Latin, French, and Math. We sat in big wicker chairs in the garden with our feet on damp gravel, our books spread out on the wooden tea table. But she was a poor scholar and would fiddle with the copper wire the gardener used to hang baskets and pots, or with her own clothing. She stopped quite soon after she started. She didn't mind that I continued. I liked Latin but found Greek and French quite difficult. Latin at least was logical and the Mathematics was do-able. I liked doing problems and figuring things out.

Susannah was full of interesting surprises. One day she said, "In 1868 Karl Marx wrote, 'Social progress can be measured exactly by the social position of the fair sex, the ugly ones included,' and he's right." I believe she did not count herself among the ugly ones, although if she hadn't had money to start with, she would have been a castoff I am sure.

She told me about a woman who became a man so that she could be a doctor. A Dr. James Barry. "Another Canadian," She said, poking me with her reading glasses, "discovered by the undertakers to be a woman, and a woman who had given birth at that. How she managed I can't think." I found out much later that this story at least was true. Dr. Barry, a woman, short, red-headed and fierce, was the first chief medical officer in the colony that became Canada.

"Women are not able to take on male occupations because of their womanly functions," said Cornelius. He had the toe of his boot on the dog's belly, rubbing her. She sprawled on her back, happy, legs spread apart. "For a few days each month, a woman must rest. What is to happen to her patients if a woman doctor is 'indisposed'? Eh?"

"Nonsense," Susannah flushed. "What about black women working in the fields. They don't lie down on those days. They continue."

Cornelius loved to tease. He teased the dogs with bits of meat and he teased Susannah, talking and joking while Susannah fussed with the spirit lamp and he pushed around the things on the mantel. Susannah was sometimes pale with pain but never took to her bed and never missed a day.

Cornelius didn't like me. Now I understand that. He frowned when he saw me unless there was someone else there, at which time he twinkled. I thought that I was doing things wrong, always wrong. I tried to stay out of his way, but that was impossible given the house routines. We met for breakfast, lunch, tea, and dinner almost every day. And often we passed at other times. So I tried to make myself small when he was around, which was difficult after Hugo came into my life because I was bursting with love. To Uncle Cornelius, I was like a slab of meat in a cold room, to be moved along on my hook in the proper order. He was not interested in me, except as a marriageable piece of property. This is strange, considering how persistently he worked to get me to England.

He grew prize-winning rhododendrons. We had to travel in a group of carriages to Wimbledon to see the rhodos in bloom there and we all had to say that his were just as fine or better. He entered his blooms in Rhododendron Society competitions, which we must attend.

He was concerned with appearances and proprieties. One of his favourite sayings was, "You weren't taught that in this house", if you did something he didn't approve of, such as skip in the hallway. He was strangely blind or tolerant of the heat between Hugo and me. He never intervened in our affair, never imposed proper chaperones, never spoke to Hugo about what he was doing. I'm glad now, even though he could have spared me much pain, I'm glad I experienced the joy of it.

Cornelius was a drunk. I didn't realize it at the time because, unlike Kate, back home, he was a very self-contained drunk. He had an interest or minor passion for collecting good Scotch whisky. Sometimes if he saw Hugo with me, he'd stand in the door of his study in a swirl of yellow dogs and call him in for a drink, even quite early in the morning. Hugo would go and I would slip away, slip back into being a child.

I have been thinking a lot about Cornelius since I started writing this some time ago. Sometimes just before I fall asleep, something comes back to me. I'm not really sure what is real and what the beginning of dreaming. He twisted my arm at the piano when I was little. He talked about prostitutes in front of the ladies. From an upper window Cornelius talking to

The Modern Age

someone in the garden. These impressions float in my mind without connecting to anything. But what I realize now is that something happened while I was in London that year I was fifteen which should have been a warning to me. It was only a shadow in the hall at night, a boy, his arms flung up.

I was actually not paying much attention, intent on my own secrets, self-absorbed. I was only fifteen and I was in love. But I wish now I had paid better attention. The boy must have been Frankie Whitehouse, a cousin on Susannah's side, whose pretty young mother came to stay when something bad was happening in her marriage. He must have been eight or ten years old. I was more interested in the mother because Hugo flirted with her and I was wary and jealous.

I don't know what happened to them, mother or son. I don't remember hearing anything about them later when I returned to London. I'm not even sure if Whitehouse was their real name or the maiden name of the mother. All I remember is this image of a shadow in the hall at night, like a Javanese puppet against the light, arm thrown up, Cornelius behind. I was in the hallway because I was sneaking downstairs to meet Hugo so that we could kiss uninterrupted in the library for an hour or two.

Now I am old like them, much older now than they were then, and I thought they were quite old. They at least had each other with whom to spar. And it turned out that Susannah adored him. Long after he was dead I visited her for a summer in London. She'd become somewhat dotty, "Where's Cornelius? Why is he always so late?"

"He's dead sweetheart," I said.

"Oh, so they tell me."

I wasn't going to write about Hugo. It's too painful. Our short but intense love affair doesn't bear on this, Zoë's story.

Except this perhaps: if I hadn't gone through all that with Hugo, if I'd loved more conventionally and married, and not had my heart broken, as they say, perhaps I'd have been kinder to Zoë, less judgmental and more fair. Perhaps she'd not be dead. She'd be here with me now, walking little dogs and sharing meals. What if what if, such a waste of time. But that is how I have come to see I must write about him. Suddenly he's on my mind so much anyway. Vivid and ruddy, laughing. It's as if I can see him again after so long.

I suppose it is common for a young lady being "finished" to look at every man she meets as a potential husband. At home, in Montreal, I'd been speaking for many years of my desire to be a doctor and had been gently indulged by my brother and Kate. I believe they were amused by my ambition and thought that if they didn't say too much I'd drop it. But I didn't. When they sent me off to England, I hid my desire and did not speak of it. I had no idea at the time of how one became a doctor. I didn't know anything about medical schools or lady doctors or what the real hardships would be. I was only fifteen.

But alongside this medical ambition, as if separated by an impermeable membrane, or in an entirely different person, lay a quite conventional interest in men and marriage. What is it Jane Austen says about that? In fact that is the whole point of the process: you are "finished" when you are married well, although no one said so and I didn't realize it at the time.

As I said, my body had gone ahead and become womanly, which I found fairly awkward on the whole. Mostly I wished to be home romping with Zoë, but then I also became quite interested in the nice feelings I had when a young man looked at me a certain way. It was embarrassing, strange, unusual, delicious. I was confused. What would it be like to be married to him? Or, is he marriageable?

I was introduced to many young men in the course of

my "coming out" but none who struck me the way Hugo did.

Susannah said, "He's quite the cheese" about Hugo before he showed up. Meaning he was well-known, well-placed, well spoken of. And well-spoken, as it turns out. She was warning me in some way, to be careful, to be charming. I don't know what.

Actually when I first saw him I thought him quite ugly. One summer evening, Hugo was standing at the fireplace mantel, frowning at the mess Cornelius had made with the knickknacks. I don't think that's what he was thinking about. He was tall enough, medium height, but had a large chest from which his front sloped gradually down to his legs. He had curly brown hair, which he wore quite long, and hazel brown eyes. We were introduced that evening but it was as if he didn't see me. Nor I him.

His hair, as I discovered later, was soft, not springy. The curls looked like they might be stiff but were actually silky and nice to touch. I came to know what his hair felt like, extraordinary, because we became engaged. I hardly know how this happened but the whole house seemed to know about it as soon as I did, with shivers down the tiles of the hallways and vibrations in the windows. Was the glass wavy before that?

I was only fifteen. In the newspapers and the halls where earnest women like my Aunt Susannah met, they were at that time debating what the age of sexual consent should be. Ten years before, in 1885, the Salvation Army had conducted a nation-wide purity campaign. They had 4,000 signatures on a petition demanding a criminal law amendment act to raise the age of sexual consent to eighteen and to give the police increased power to search and arrest brothel keepers. They had a document two and a half miles long, drawn in a wagon to the House of Commons by cadets from Clapham Training Home. Over the cart was a white canopy reading: "In the name of the people and the Queen, mother of the country, the Salvation Army demand that iniquity shall cease." This petition, accompanied by 300 uniformed women soldiers of the Army, made its way along a route filled with crowds. Susannah told me all about it complete with clippings from the newspaper.

For me, from my experience, fifteen is old enough to have uncontainable sexual feelings. Or perhaps I should say barely containable. The social restraints, the idea of what a lady was, the taboos and holdings back, restrained us, so that an early pregnancy was never a danger, nor contracting disease. I am grateful now for that. At the time I was almost insane with disdain for the social system that would not leave me alone with him in a room so we could explore each other's bodies. And yet I was also aware from my long habit of eavesdropping that there were scandals and court cases concerning women, wives, who had been given syphilis by their bounder husbands. What a blessing antibiotics have been really. Although there are those who would argue that fear of disease is the only thing that held the moral fabric together. I say let it unravel then.

I believe the laws and the debate around the age of sexual consent are meant mostly to govern the actions of the lower classes where social strictures are not enforced. And now, now it is 1964, it seems from what I can pick up that there are no social strictures around sexuality. Well at least my nieces don't have to worry about getting pregnant. I will have to add this to the list of things about which I am now unable to form an opinion.

It is not an original observation that repression increases sexual charge. However I can report this from direct experience. Hugo and I found ways to touch each other. His fingers trailed for a second along the soft skin of the inside of my forearm. Mine brushed for a few seconds through his soft hair. Then, when we became engaged, we believed that we had received a license to kiss. So we kissed a great deal, mostly outdoors slowly, but also quickly in hallways and briefly empty rooms. He had the loveliest lips. I am still a creature of my time, and subject to its shame I guess, since I feel I can write this only as a relief to myself, not as something anyone will ever look at. I shall edit this away later: his lips were delicious, large and sweet and sensitive. When we kissed it was a new language, something he brought me from a tropical place or the desert and infused in my nerves. I was languid and receptive, agreeable, and energized with a wild energy. I would want to arm wrestle, climb trees, slide banisters. One time his hand slid along my stomach for a second as if by accident and I experienced a violent lurch in my being.

I am a small person and I always have been. And Hugo's hands were large, smooth-skinned, articulate. It was wonderful to put my small body into those large hands.

"You know you're alive because you can feel your heart beat," Hugo said. The first time you feel someone else's heart beat and know another is alive too.

Or when you are really frightened and you know you are really alive. "Really, really alive," said Hugo.

He was a traveler, an explorer, when there were still places to explore. How he managed to mount his expeditions I don't know. I think he had money of his own, and he raised money from private subscriptions. He was often off to speak at Oxford or at a house party in the country. He sought places and situations that made his heart beat faster.

What is it in me that has, since then, sought out situations that made my heart feel sore? Not racing, but slowed, a deliberately calm beat, but sore, even with my hands in another's body or lifting a baby from a vagina. Breastbone aching, bone bruise sore. How did I doctor all the years, most of what I did useless against the pain except for morphia? Well, enough of the self-pitying note.

The first time Hugo and I really looked at each other, I was in the Holland Street garden, up in the Queen Ann cherry tree, sitting with my feet hanging down, eating cherries. He saw me and bowed. I bowed back. Then we grinned. After that, he was often around and attentive to me. I suppose I was starved for attention and he was easy to talk to. His eyes were light, golden or brown, or greenish, and he looked at me and smiled. I smiled back. I couldn't stop myself. I didn't know how. I was fifteen, a young fifteen. He was twenty-two and worldly. I was no match for him.

Once he returned from some weeks away and we were kissing in the hallway and I slipped my hand into his pocket and there was sand.

"Oh yes, that's for you," Hugo said.

He would say, "We'll get married after you finish medical school."

"And where shall we live?"

"In a small town in Canada."

It was a game we played, a teasing flirting game. I had no way of knowing he didn't mean it.

"We shall get married and have six children and you will raise them up."

"What about my practise?"

"Oh we shall have wonderful nurses to help with the children."

When I went back to my house, my brother's house, in Canada, we corresponded. His letters were short and highly descriptive. I wish I could find them now, but they seem to have disappeared, long gone I suppose. You'd think that would be the kind of thing I'd hang on to, but no. Perhaps I destroyed them in a blank fit of pain. I don't remember doing that, but it seems likely. What I do recall is the excitement each of these short bright missives brought me. Mostly he sent postcards, each a small window on a completely different world: a humourous story about bargaining for a carpet in the market in

The Modern Age

Istanbul on the European side, not the Asian; an orchid hunting expedition in Central America deep in bright forest with vines and birds screeching; a self-deprecating story about being sick in a lurching ship. I could see each place in my mind's eye.

I wrote to him about my world, my animals, Zoë, the weather. It never occurred to me that, to him, I was also exotic. But perhaps that explains it. A feisty colonial girl, more sensual and closer to the earth than the over-bred British girls. Perhaps it was something like that. And young. The closer we got to marriage, to convention, to grown-up life, the farther he ran. How else to explain?

But why explain at all? It doesn't matter, except to understand how all this changed me and made me mean and hard hearted towards Zoë.

Hugo said he was a Sufi but I did not then, and do not now, know what that means. He spoke often of being free.

Hugo sat with me in the cherry tree, our shoes off, and sang a song which he made up:

Yes to grape leaves fat and serrated, light and dark dappled green.

Yes to the strength of the trunk of the grape twisting in curves of gray brown and, yes to deep pink under peeling bark.

Yes to long branches of grape stretching for sun, to curling reaching pale tendrils.

Yes to incipient grapes.

Yes to phlox in brilliant pink masses.

Yes to delicate pink of geraniums.

Yes to chive and branching fennel.

Yes even to aphid and black angelica seed heads, yes.

And then he kissed me.

He and I sometimes pretended we were children and played Cowboys and Indians in the large garden. Once he tied me up to a tree and ran away for a long time.

When I went back to London almost five years later, I didn't feel like I'd grown-up at all though I know I looked different, womanly instead of girlish. Five years of daydreaming about our life together, thinking he might even come to Canada to see me. When I returned after my brother died, Hugo looked the same, but he'd traveled more and gathered more. He'd made a home for himself. He seemed to have figured out who he was. Later I was jilted. I was engaged and then he left me. He sent me The Orchid-Grower's Manual. And the orchids themselves. But I didn't see him again after that.

Sun shines through glass now on my head and thinning hair, and at eighty-four I know that it is possible to be happy with very little. But then, I was wild with happiness, throbbing with it, vibrating.

I have just come in breathless from walking the dog and, without even taking off my coat, wonder how I can never have noticed before that the first colour of spring, the first sign of the only resurrection that I acknowledge anymore, is red. Zoë's colour. The deep brilliant red of the what? dogwood, or willow stems along the railway tracks. Here I am. I've written too much about myself. I've written about Hugo and Cornelius and Susannah. But hardly anything about Zoë, who was who I wanted to write about. I close my eyes and colours swirl behind them and those colours are Zoë, red swirls. I do not know the names of the trees that have made the first colour.

Zoë in the cherry tree in a red dress laughing.

The Modern Age

Zoë on her father's shoulders before he died.

Zoë in London later, lying on the hearth rugs with Cornelius's dogs, pretending to be a dog, responding to prods with the toe and belly rubs, but not to words.

Merry little girl and sullen. One or the other, black and white, or red and blue.

"She's so like her mother," said Cornelius, shaking his head judgmentally. I could tell he meant it was bad to be like Kate. I wondered whether he really knew her at all.

"I'm a New Woman," Zoë said when she was ten or eleven, after we were in London, in Cornelius's house, her hands on her hips in a most unladylike way. She was the first in our household to put on bloomers and ride a bicycle. She wheedled it out of Cornelius. Determined to have her way. It was completely different being there the second time with Zoë.

Zoë asking questions of Hugo. She had thousands of questions.

She was striking always with dark brown eyes, fair skin and light hair.

"Zoë Zoë mebowey fee fi fa fowee, Zoë."

Zoë streaking through the little park across the street on Holland Street. Athletic, energetic.

Concentrated energy like sunlight through a magnifying glass

Willful, indulged. "I won't I won't." Who took the brunt of it?

Kicking the dogs.

"I'm a New Woman and I want to be called Patrick from now on."

Later she was like a D.H. Lawrence woman in bright clashing colours with brilliant stockings. But then, Hugo brought us boys' clothes and snuck us out into the world. It was easy to pass as a boy then because women's fashions were so exaggerated. We had to keep our hats on because our hair was still long so we mostly stayed outside. It was a lark. Later when I did it in deadly earnest, I cut my hair off. "Your beautiful hair," said Zoë, the so-called New Woman. It had snowed surprisingly and the light of it reflected into the room in a pleasing glow. "Everything's changed. Everything's changed," she said, arms spread at the window, exulting. But I hadn't told her yet that I was leaving her.

It's as if the raging moods of youth are on me again. Yesterday I felt so sad and wrote so wildly all out of order. Today, this morning anyway, I am calm. I will continue this story properly, with things in the right order.

The next thing would be the party on New Year's Eve, 1899 to 1900.

FOUR

On January 1, 1900, my brother and guardian, George, and his wife, Kate, died in a crash of their Stanley Steamer. Kate was driving and was almost certainly intoxicated. They left their own party laughing just after midnight. Many guests were still there, not dancing anymore but drinking, laughing, sitting talking, flirting.

Well go back: when I returned to Canada at the end of the year in London, engaged and swollen with Hugo's kisses, life returned to its quiet ways. I studied quite seriously for several years with a proper tutor, a man this time. Zoë was

The Modern Age

growing and she spent more time on schoolwork too. I longed for Hugo and treasured his postcards. I longed for the time when I would be old enough and we could be together. Missing Hugo, longing for the mail to come every day, I was happy, because I believed that we would marry and be happy, that I would go to medical school and perhaps on to Vienna to study with this interesting new man, Freud. Anything was possible. We were coming up to a new century. But missing Hugo put me out of the present and I suppose in some ways I was never really happy again. Anyway, the time passed quickly.

The party was Kate's idea. Something big and lavish to celebrate the new century, the new age. My sister-in-law Kate was always eager to push into the new. She was cheeky, cocky. She wanted to throw a big party. Fancy food, extra servants, musicians. And she got all that. The preparations went on for weeks. Kate wanted electric candles like flames in sconces all along the walls of the ballroom and she struggled with workmen to get it done in time. The house was turned upside down with cleaning. The cooking went on and on. The cooler was full of good things. Zoë and I would sneak in and pick at the edges of roasts, poke our fingers into puddings. I was too old for this, childish, even though nineteen already. Kate caught us and slapped our hands, but she was laughing.

We had many fittings for our dresses. Kate's was petals of lemon coloured silk embroidered with seed pearls along the edges of each petal. Mine was a simple dark green silk to be worn with Kate's jade pendant. And Zoë's was brilliant red of course, against the wishes of her mother and the astonishment of the dressmaker.

And the party was fabulous. We were all beautiful, fabulous flowers, with men as the dark stems. We danced. It was a dream, a delight. We ate like gluttons all the food we had nibbled before. We drank.

I heard someone say, "It must have cost a fortune," and turned to see who it was but there was no one behind me. I turned back and heard, "Her family has pots of money." There was some kind of acoustic anomaly so that I could hear people talking from across the room as if they were right behind me.

We danced. Men smelled of cigars, which they smoked on the porch in the cold air then they came in with ice on their moustaches and swirled us up into the dance. An old man with strong alcohol breath and wet whiskers kissed me. I was shocked and pulled away. Repulsion. How could kisses be so different? He reminded me of Uncle Cornelius. Maybe Susannah liked those husband kisses. I could only imagine hating them. But the disgust slid away in a blur of champagne. We were giddy and brilliant. The room filled with hot laughter.

Just before midnight, the band stopped playing and someone started a series of toasts, which got wilder and wilder. The servants went around with champagne bottles and refilled glasses quickly as Kate egged them on. We toasted the New Year, Kate and George, the electric candles, the Age of Electricity, the champagne, the French Revolution, and the Bank of Montreal. Near me a man raised his glass and called out, "To rationality, science, and the new objectivity."

"To rationality, science, and the new objectivity," we all caroled back.

Suddenly I was raising my glass and calling out, "To women's suffrage." I wasn't too drunk to notice the little pause as people wondered whether they could really drink to that, and the 'what the hell' spirit in which they called back raggedly, "To women's suffrage."

Then we drank to tramways ("To tramways"), to subways ("subways"). To the Budapest subway, the Paris subway, the Boston subway, and the great and amazing London Underground.

"The great and amazing London Underground!"

Finally, just before midnight, my brother, George called out, "To the Modern Age."

The Modern Age

We raised our glasses solemnly and repeated slowly, "The Modern Age."

George and Kate went off just after midnight, laughing, in the new Stanley Steamer he'd given her for Christmas. When they left he was driving. He was drunk but not too bad. When they found them frozen, where the car had run into a snow bank on the frozen river, Kate was in the driver's seat.

But there was a strange lull of twelve hours. It was not until after noon the next day that someone came to the door. We just didn't know where they were. They could have taken a hotel room in the city or driven all the way to New York for all we knew. In fact they'd driven out the wagon road onto the ice of the river.

Kate and George gone. In the nine years since my father's death I'd just gotten to accept life, to be like any nineteen-year-old who feels immortal. My brother, his sweetness gone, his body frozen. Fortunately someone else took care of that part. Although now I'm not squeamish about bodies, it amazes me how others took care of things.

The news came to us in the winter garden where we were playing with the new camera. Zoë had made me stand still and get my picture taken. I'm smiling despite the champagne hangover because she was wearing a habitant cap and her face was radiant in the bright winter light. There's a photo of her, also smiling, without the cap, but in a dark coat with fur around the wrists and collar. I seem to recall that the coat was burgundy. She was tall for her age. I was wearing a gray fitted coat with blue velvet appliqué. I loved that coat. We both sparkle in the sunshine. How young I was even for nineteen. After that the darkness came down swift as the end of the winter day.

I don't remember who came to the door, who dealt with it. The pictures were taken just before shock set in and the camera lost thereafter. The pictures came to us in London later. Caught in the journey, paused. Shaken but the news had not reached the brain yet and gone out to the body.

Who dealt with it? The car flung hard against the snow bank, the frozen bodies, the funeral, the house, the servants, Zoë and I two underage females? Uncle Cornelius from a distance, I suppose, but who took care of the details? Who booked our passage and arranged for us to be watched by a Mrs. Armitage across the Atlantic? Who told us that's what we were doing? I'm sure I can remember if I try hard enough, but there is blackness around those memories, Zoë only shining out of them. Zoë hysterical and flinging herself around, then going stony and cold, scaring me.

I stayed focused on Zoë, on taking care of her and everything else in that time is a blur. But one night, late, after she had finally gotten off to sleep, I went into my brother's room and sat on the end of their marital bed for a long time. Then, as if drawn by some force, I found myself in his dressing room, with my kerosene lamp throwing a soft light onto his clothes. There was one suit of his I had always liked the feel of. The wool was softer, maybe cashmere, and the colour a dark charcoal, almost black. I found that suit by running my hands along the clothes with my eyes shut. I was as if bewitched. I pulled off my dressing gown and nightgown and pulled on the suit pants. I'm small, but my brother was also small. I found that by turning over the waistband, I could make the pants fit. I liked the feel of the soft wool against my legs. I found a shirt and put that on, and a tie. I found suspenders and put them on, hitching up the pants a bit more. I found cufflinks on the dresser, a pair of his black socks in a drawer, and garters. I put on the suit jacket. I stood for a long time in front of the full-length mirror as if in a dream. My hair was loose around my shoulders so I looked truly strange, neither man nor woman. I turned and pulled my hair back. I shook it out again. I crouched down like a man on a lawn. I stood again. There was the sound of a door shutting somewhere else in the house. I grabbed my nightgown and robe and stuffed them under my arm. I picked up a pair of black boots in one hand and the kerosene lamp in the other. Then I half-ran, half-walked, with caution not to lose the glass cover of the lamp, back to my own room. I closed the door softly and then undressed without looking in my own mirror. I carefully folded up my brother's clothes and put them in the bottom of the steamer trunk opened against the wall, which had been put there three days before for me to pack for London. I didn't want to pack, but that night I did, covering the dark soft suit with layers of my dresses and underwear and stockings and shoes carefully packed in tissue paper. I packed in a fever all that night and the next day, without sleep, packed Zoë too. We left on a steamship three days after that. We were so sick.

I'm going to die. Quite soon probably. I'm healthy now but frail. Breathing is getting more difficult and anything could take me any minute. Not many women live past eighty. I'm nothing special so I'm probably going to die soon. If there is terror at that, it's come soft-pawed into the room and is sitting quietly looking out the window. I feel just well enough to try to get this down and not too concerned if I don't. Well yes, tell the truth, concerned, driven in fact. It seems beyond my powers to finish this as I am often weak and tired, but I drive on. I doubt that anyone will notice one way or another. But what's this? I seem to have some small intense desire to catch that mouse, to tell how hard it was, how sad. Some pedagogical purpose. So strange.

My nephew and his wife have brought me an alarm clock, which they say I must set for meal times. I'm forgetting to eat. I seem not to be hungry anymore and am growing very thin. But if I can't remember to eat, how can I remember to set the alarm clock? These young people are very silly sometimes but they seem worried so I will lie to them more convincingly.

Stupid. Go on.

So these New Year deaths were also the end of my childhood, the end of my freedom as an orphan. Zoë and I were passed like furniture into the care of Uncle Cornelius. Apparently this was a legal transfer of items carried out by lawyers in Montreal and London, using the telegraph. Zoë and I found ourselves on a ship bound for London, without being consulted, without notice, even though I was almost twenty by then. Orphans under orders. We were both sick the whole time, throwing up in the tiny cabin and making it stink.

All this happened so fast, a long slide into helplessness. Kate's family was no help. Later with Zoë's child, they were so insistent, at such a cost to me. Maybe because they regretted letting Zoë go, as I did. Anyway, Cornelius was finally in charge. Once, twice, third time he got us. He arranged the berth, the attendance of a woman in the next cabin, for Aunt Susannah to meet us and for us to come up on the train. He was the one who sold up the house in Montreal. Why couldn't we have stayed there? It was never a possibility. And Zoë and I were too light, too flimsy to protest. We had no idea. We were blown across the ocean by the male force of this man who knew what was best for us.

FIVE

We were shipped seasick in a violent storm the whole way, and heartsick, from Montreal to Southampton and on to London. Shipped like the goods that our families had shipped from Antigua, Montreal, Barbados. The ugly truth is that part of me exulted right through the grief, right through the six day crossing, exulted while I held Zoë's hand as she moaned and threw up, and even while I threw up. I exulted because I would see Hugo; I was going to England to see Hugo, and exulted right through the guilt at feeling this in such a terrible time. By the end of January the Montreal house was packed up and sold and we were settled in the big house in Holland Street with

The Modern Age

Cornelius and Susannah.

At first I waited eagerly every day to see Hugo. I went eagerly down to breakfast thinking he may have arrived in the night. I dressed carefully for dinner thinking tonight he may be among the guests. No one mentioned him. I seemed to be the only one who remembered that we were engaged. I wrote letters to the last address I had for him and listened twice a day for the click of the mailbox, forcing myself to walk slowly down to the front door, putting one slipper in front of the other. But there was no response. I started to get a sick feeling, a churning in the pit of my stomach. I was afraid to ask Aunt Susannah about him. She was preoccupied with Women's Suffrage meetings and petitions. I was very alone, but I was used to that. I would have talked to Zoë but she was not doing well.

The first time Zoë suffered nightmares, or night terrors, she screamed so loudly that I was sure the whole house would awaken. But I was the only one who came. My room was next door; perhaps they didn't hear. But it was not just one scream; it was a long series of shrieks that went on and on as I fumbled to light a lamp. When I got to her, her arms were outstretched with her palms out, as if warding something off. Her eyes were open but she was not awake. "Zoë Zoë," I called, but she went on shrieking. I put my arms around her shoulders. She was cold and damp with sweat. I kept talking below the screams, saying her name and, "It's all right. It's all right." After a while, the screams turned to sobs and her body became less rigid. She lay down and turned away on her side, never waking up or knowing I was there. I covered her shoulders and went back to my own room. But I didn't sleep. After that first time, I had the sense that the household was awake, listening, waiting for her screams to subside, while I fumbled with lamps and robes and useless words. What is the purpose of nightmares? To wake you up. I didn't awaken.

We were not happy. She had one of these bad times once or twice a week and the weeks went by. London was cold and damp and dark. I came to believe that Hugo would never come. Cornelius was drinking heavily.

One day, Susannah came around the corner with a sheaf of papers in her hand just as Zoë and I were running down the curved stairs into the hall. Susannah gathered herself to attention from the papers and squinted at us as we tried to pull ourselves together. Obviously whatever we had been in Canada was not quite up to snuff. There was remedial work to be done. She went back into the morning room and beckoned us to follow her, then sat at the Buhl roll-top desk that stood by the window and wrote a series of notes, dipping her pen in the china inkwell with its intricate flower design and pale colours while Zoë and I perched on the lumpy day bed, watching as though tranced. There were rocks shining in a crystal bowl in the morning room. Susannah was always picking up rocks. She had them in jars pickled in vinegar to make them shine.

As a result of Susannah's notes, I was thrown into a group of young ladies who went around visiting each other in packs. Susannah insisted. In her tense compact way she said I mustn't mope, without referring directly to Hugo. I felt that she could see right through me and found me wanting, felt sometimes she was cold and unemotional. Susannah seemed unresponsive but she was also hypersensitive to rejection. She had no small talk, not a word of wasted chat. When she said something or gave an instruction, she only said it once, but she did not stay focused on anything except her Women's Suffrage.

The young women Susannah introduced me to were interested mostly in fashion and gossip. They had small waists and big hair and soon I did too. We wore long sleeves, with lots of extra fabric in the big dresses. I scanned the group each time we met, hoping that one could be a friend but it did not turn out that way and I continued to be lonely.

They felt a need to instruct me. I was driving with two of them in a wagonette and one said grandly, "And that is Lord's cricket grounds."

I said, joking, "Is that where the Lords play cricket?"

"Oh you Americans."

"I'm Canadian."

"It's all the same."

Obviously I was expected to be a bit rough. That served me well later when I was working with the orchids and secretly saving money to go to medical school. I've sat for a long time here at my desk trying to remember those girls' names, but I can't.

I felt I was above the young ladies to whom Susannah introduced me because I was studying medicine, even though I wasn't actually studying at the time. I was a scientist, baffled by being a woman scientist but Susannah encouraged me to think that that was changing. I had a straight line to the future. Two-sided, the baby me, playing with Zoë and being irresponsible. And scientist me, the one who believed in progress, in the cure for syphilis and tuberculosis. It was 1900 and I believed in Evolution. I had read Darwin and his system seemed to fit quite well with my leftover Hindoo belief in reincarnation.

I came back from these bouts with the young ladies and told Zoë all about them including all the gossip. Zoë was amused and made rude comments. But Susannah's interest in making ladies of us waned quickly. The engagements had a life of their own and continued, but Zoë and I were allowed to slip back into our lives in which I pretended I was a child playing with Zoë while I secretly waited for Hugo. I spent many hours sitting for Zoë as she did my portrait over and over again in pastels and oils and crayon and pencil. I don't remember how Zoë got all these materials. But I vividly remember the slope-ceilinged room at the top of the house in which we did this and her intense concentration, her head bowed into a pool of light with the long dark braid down her back and pastel dust or oil paint all around her, and the pleasurable feeling, almost sexual, of sitting for a portrait. I wonder what happened to those portraits in which I looked out a bit prim with big eyes. The portraits changed too, became strange and extremely vivid with purples and reds, but still recognizably me. Nowhere to be found now.

Looking back I can see that I was afraid of Cornelius. That fear kept me frozen for a long time. That and my absolute conviction that Hugo was coming back to me. I had the ambition to be a doctor. I was almost twenty years old. And I did nothing. I spent many hours with empty eyes, dreaming. In one dream I was in the hot hills of Haiti as a doctor, helping poor people. "I get the urge for going but I never seem to go," I told Zoë.

Zoë's plan for me was that we would progress through my dreams together, she would be an artist and I a doctor and all would be well. I liked that dream well enough -- it supported my inaction. I called myself lazy and shiftless but, shining the long light of hindsight on myself as I was then, I think I was mostly afraid. Cornelius was drinking and would turn sullen by the end of dinner and much wine. I have not turned out to be a lazy person.

In the meantime, Aunt Susannah was giving me two stories at once. On the one hand she said, explicitly, be a woman, be yourself. On the other, she said, a bit more underhandedly, be society's woman, get married.

This all came clear to me, and my desperation overcame my fear one day in early March. It was the day that the Canadians had announced they were going in to the Boer War. Cornelius crowed at breakfast. He felt he knew something about Canada. It felt more like June than March, muggy and overcast. Zoë was down at the end of the garden drawing in the bamboo. She was wearing a pale green skirt and jacket, which caused her almost to disappear in the thicket. I was up in a flowering cherry, lost in blossoms, hands caressing the satin bark, my skirt gathered around my legs and my back comfortable against the big trunk. I heard Susannah before I saw her and she was talking about me.

"Oh dear. How shall we ever get Mary-Margaret married when she acts so glum and plays at being a baby?" I should have swung down then but I sat still instead.

"Marriage is a form of prostitution." It was the high harsh voice of one of her suffrage cronies. "Haven't you said that yourself?"

Susannah laughed "Yes, oh yes I've said that. Woman is a many-splendoured thing. Yes?" I couldn't see them but I could tell they were sitting down at the tea table under the brilliant arch of forthysia in the next walkway, smoking cigarettes. Their voices were strangely clear; the day was still. "But she's so hapless. It's for her own good. She was a bright thing at fifteen but she's so moony now."

"What about the little one?"

"Oh she amuses Cornelius." At the time that did not seem sinister to me.

"Doesn't Mary-Margaret have a good deal of money?"

"Oh yes. I suppose we could just wait and things would take care of themselves."

"Terrible toothache," said the high-pitched voice. Mrs. French was her name. She was a tiny woman with strong convictions and an apparently indulgent husband.

Susannah made a sympathetic sound but she was clearly preoccupied with my failures. "I'm hoping our little Nigel will propose and take her off to India."

Nigel was an officer in the Indian army, on leave, and spending a great deal of time at our dinner table. He told me once at dinner that the Indian army was the place to be because you had so much leisure. I tried, and could not imagine, at what he spent his leisure in hot India. He wore tight-fitting and strangely bright clothes and didn't seem to care that he gave every appearance of liking men rather than women. I was appalled that my sensible Aunt Susannah would consider sending me off to India with him. Did I make up Hugo? Was I so deluded? My heart closed into a tight fist in my chest.

I'd been asleep, deep in an unhappy doze, unaware of all that was going on around me. That afternoon, Nigel came to tea and Susannah took Zoë off on a pretend errand. I was trapped in the hot room with the perspiring young man. The horror of it is indescribable. Someday I will tell my nieces how lucky they are that men and women don't feel obliged to do this kind of thing any more. To my own credit, I was able to say, "You don't like me."

"I do not think of you at all in that light," he said, entirely forging his passport. Honour. A life that would be respectable if I let him go his own way and shielded him from society's gaze. That's what he seemed to be offering. In India. That part intrigued me but I said no. "No, dear boy. Have a real life." I never found out if he did or not. This was the year that Oscar Wilde died after his terrible gaol ordeal.

I ran out of the room and went to a far bench in the garden and sat while it got dark. I did not cry. I never cried. I decided to talk to Cornelius that night about medical school and to get on with my life. Give up on Hugo. Be damned with it.

When the crash happened, the death of my brother and the smashing of our lives, I'd been languidly getting ready to go to Vienna and start medical studies there. Or somewhere. Perhaps I hadn't really figured out the details. I was afraid and that made me languid. Before our lives fell apart, I was focused mainly on being nearer to Hugo. Maybe Edinburgh. I wasn't even clear yet on which medical schools took women. Now I didn't know where Hugo was to be near.

I was back in the living room early, dressed for dinner with my courage screwed up. Cornelius had his drink and was standing by the mantel. I didn't know for sure I was going to do it just then; the words just came out of my mouth. I had to look up at Cornelius -- he was much taller than I was -- "I'm going to medical school as soon as it can be arranged."

Cornelius laughed and turned red, pursing his large puffy lips. "Ladies are not doctors, my dear. In fact, is that not an oxymoron?" he demanded, looking across at Susannah for confirmation because he was uneasy with words. She just pursed her own thin lips and shook her head. "Oxymoron? Lady doctor?" He laughed again with his hand over his mouth, threw back the whisky and swept us in to dinner, putting that same hand on the small of my back as we went in.

If I had another life perhaps I would try to understand these currents of revulsion or attraction between people. My uncle's hand on the small of my back made me cold, as if, speaking medically, all the blood had retreated to protect the inner organs. It surprised me, that big rubbery flipper on the thin fabric over my back; I even turned to see what it was. His touch caused me to shrivel, chilled to the bone, smaller than small, helpless. I'm way beyond medical description here. The opposite indeed of what I remembered of Hugo's glancing touch along my forearm. Now Zoë's night terrors come back to me somehow.

Zoë and I had been separated, I declared an adult, and made to eat with the adults, she to the nursery like a proper British child, and then to bed. I missed her by my shoulder and under my arm at dinner. I missed her quickness, her laugh, and her wit. After dinner I went into her bedroom and told her that Cornelius said I must not be a lady doctor because you couldn't be both, lady and doctor. I was hard and dry. I didn't cry. Zoë said, "Oh be a doctor. Being a lady looks so tiresome."

That was the first time of asking.

We had another nasty scene the next morning. At breakfast Cornelius said, "Come with me please." He scared me. Once when I was there at fifteen, Hugo came to me by the fire one night after Susannah and I had left the men to their port and then they came in. He shook his head and said in a low voice, "Cornelius is vile." I thought that was normal. All families have this. Hugo never said any more. But that's what I thought as Cornelius beckoned to me, Cornelius is vile.

I got up to follow and he ushered me in to his study which I'd hardly been inside before, though I had peeped in though the glass door with its leaded windows when he was out of the house. It was dark after the bright breakfast room. There was a fire in the grate and a vase of daffodils on the edge of his green leather topped desk and a green letter opener and an open box with pens in it. He nodded to the straight chair across the desk from him and waited while I sat. Then he sat on his own green leather swivel chair and opened a drawer. He drew out a large cigar, which he lit slowly and carefully while I waited. Then after a long inhale and exhale of vile smoke he said, "Now then." He reached into the desk again and put a piece of paper in front of me, turning it towards me, meant for me to read.

On the thick creamy paper was the name of an extremely popular patent medicine. Then the words: Receipt. Recipe. Rx, written in brown ink. Then a list of ingredients, including sugar, alcohol, and some common herbs. I felt contempt and the sense of a blow to the Solar plexus.

"This is the source of your wealth, young lady," he said, pausing to inhale and exhale again. "When you are twenty-five you can do what you like with it. In the meantime I control it. I make money from your money and you do too. Your father trusted me to make money and your brother did too. I trust you will continue to trust me. However, as I say, when you are twenty-five you may do as you like. I hope you never forget that all this is thanks to the credulity of sick people. That will do." He nodded to the door and I got up and left.

I had never thought really about money, about where the comforts and servants had come from. We were the new rich, the new middle class, getting up by stripping the colonies of their wealth. Or serving those who were stripping the colonies. I didn't know until then that I had personal wealth, which I was not to have access to until I was twenty-five. I didn't know that there was money on my father's side. I never thought about it until I wanted to do something and I couldn't because Uncle Cornelius controlled the money. I had always thought my father was a humble physician, which he was, and the son of a humble physician before him. But it turned out that his father, besides being a physician, had invented and very successfully marketed this patent medicine, which was still selling. Or maybe I knew about the patent medicine and had forgotten.

SIX

The next day I was totally turned around again: a card from Hugo in the early mail. Hugo had written from Cornwall. It turned out to be the first of a series of enigmatic cards. I was back to living from one mail delivery to another. I didn't even think about medical school. Why bother?

On one of the cards Hugo wrote, "The gorse is bursting into golden flame." And on another, "In Cornwall, the sky never grows dark, the darkness seems to come welling up out of the earth like dye." Hugo was intense, as if he was breathing oxygen instead of air. He had a passionate love of nature. I kept turning the cards over, looking at the address. Yes he knew I was here in Holland Street in London. He didn't say when he would see me, or what he was doing. It was agony.

Those few weeks I spent waiting for Hugo were such a small part of this long life but they made a deep mark on me. Maybe the mark was already there and the hurting he gave me just found the old hurt and carved it a bit deeper. But it was at that time, at the age of nineteen, that I decided not ever to be dependent on another person. Eventually I let die the faint hope of meeting a man whom I could be with as I was with Hugo. But that experience, being with Hugo, was like a pressed flower imperceptibly fading in a hidden book, rarely opened, and now when I turn to that page, faint colours crumbling and a few silken petals remaining. I was pressed flat to longing, so that became my state, always longing for something. Hugo told Zoë in response to one of her thousand questions that longing was good, the more longing the better. I didn't, and still don't, understand.

And still, after all this resolve and stiffening, when he finally arrived one morning I trembled and acted like a goose.

"Where were you?" I tried to keep my voice steady, to keep it from accusing, from having any feeling at all. Now, sixty-five years later, I realize I was angry.

"Oh off polishing my heart. Did you miss me?"

I nodded helplessly. He was so calm and collected, so enigmatic. He was there in the bright doorway one morning in early April. He was there, his brown eyes bright and merry. Brilliant red tulips trembled along the walk behind him. I stepped out of the dim hallway into the sunlight and closed the heavy door behind us. He took my hands in his and, in full view of the street, kissed me on the lips.

I pulled away and hung my head like a maiden in a story. I was breathless and my heart beat hard. I remember wondering if this was how my mother felt when they put electric current through her body.

Insha'Allah Allah willing. That's what Hugo used to say. My lover was a Sufi, a traveler. He brought me things -- ideas, robes, diseases possibly. Was he psychopathic? Did he die? Or just disappear? What did he look like? Thick hip bones on mine. Wiry strong. He lifts me up. He comes back from the desert with face and hands brown, other skin white. Hair. He is gritty, smoothed by sand. There is a small sift of sand in the pocket of one of his jackets and a bit of dried plant. He brings back desert medicines and laughs at my chemicals, at my family crest, at my grandfather who made a patent medicine. I am ashamed. Shame and love. Time passes so quickly. The feel of his rough cheek in my palm. My face against his. His hand on my stomach. He is not sociable, and he does dinner parties. He is aloof and reserved, and he flirts outrageously. I am afraid, seeing him with other women. Maybe he sleeps with many women. Perhaps he brings disease. I'd be forced to take a cure, which would nearly kill me. He is gone for six months and then here again. The war comes. He dies. I am alone for so many years but the days pass quickly whether I think of him or not, or whether I think I am thinking of him for I always am. I just don't always notice it. As if he could be coming back, still coming back. I don't believe in his death. I can't accept the permanence of it. Still coming back.

He took me up again. It was different than it had been when I first met him. Now I was older, I could go about more and Susannah was careless about chaperoning me. It was considered enough for Zoë to chaperone us and we went about a great deal as a threesome, Zoë playing the gooseberry and asking questions flirtatiously. Hugo took us places we never would have gone otherwise. The Cafe Royal with its marble tables, glittering decoration, and raucous men where we ate Macaroni au Gratin, disregarding all the other interesting things written in French on the menu like Pigeon de Bordeaux and Canard Sauvage. I met the composer Peter Warlock there but couldn't hear what he said across the table due to the clatter of dominoes. Peter Warlock later put the cat out, locked the door, and turned on the gas. This was after Zoë's suicide. After the Crash and Cornelius's death. So I heard with a heart hardened by all these things. But between the time that I saw him there at the Café Royale and the time he died, he composed a number of lovely songs, some of which I have on recordings and play from time to time as if they could bring back an afternoon spent with Hugo across the table from a composer.

At the Café Royale, were painters and alleged spies and society women. Zoë loved it. She was a bohemian at heart. D.H. Lawrence was there at the same time apparently, asking, "What do you think of yourself?" "Do you love your wife?" But we didn't meet him. There were women in yellow silk and with patent leather shoes. It was a place where the big debates of the age were on, and out in the open. "How much better this world would be if we weren't so shy about going in here and there," said one of the young men who was a believer in Empire. "How much better if our culture became their culture. They would learn to thank us."

"All men have the right to be free," said Hugo. He was always somewhat enigmatic and did not engage directly in the debate though I thought I knew what he was thinking.

Then this: one day soon after he returned, Hugo announced we were going bicycling in the country. At tea time when only Zoë and I were in the room he knelt and took off my shoe then measured my stocking foot with his large hands. I shivered.

We met at Kings Cross and Hugo took us to a village near East Grinstead where some friends of his had a cottage. He brought men's clothing for Zoë and me. We went upstairs with the rough tweeds and subdued colours in our hands and came back down with them covering our loosened bodies and with our hair tucked up into soft hats. For the second time in my life I put on pants and for the first time went out in them. What freedom! Clothing that lets the air in. It was like swimming naked, which I later did at night at Mrs. Blaylock's place on the Sunshine Coast. You could move, kick, jump. Zoë was ecstatic. Soon she was begging Susannah for bloomers and a bicycle and when she had her own money and her independence she always wore trousers. Now I do too. I'm sure the neighbours think I'm a queer old duck.

Hugo's friends were away in France so we played house in their cottage. It was raining when we arrived, then the sun came out. We made coffee in the kitchen and carried kitchen chairs out into the garden where we ate the bread and cheese and sausage that Hugo had brought. Hugo's friends had many bicycles in a dim shed in the garden. Hugo found two that were small enough for us and wheeled them out. We fell off laughing many times in the cottage yard while Hugo tried to hold us up. Then, surprisingly quickly, we were flying along the lane, hair unsnagging from our hats and trailing out. Then uphill, puffing, red-faced. It was so much fun. We soared down the lanes over the dusty, packed earth, between the aromatic hedges. Women free in their bodies, flying. This was the Modern Age. The wild roses were not quite out and their smell mingled with the smell of dirt after rain.

However, a nasty incident cast a shadow on an otherwise glorious day. Zoë was sailing along in front; Hugo and I were riding slowly, talking. At the bottom of a hill, a group of people had gathered in the lane. Zoë tried to avoid them, wobbled, and knocked over an old man. We came up quickly, and laid down our bikes. The man was surrounded by the small crowd, all speaking a foreign language. His face constricted in pain and he tried to open it to show he wasn't hurt but he was. Zoë was still trying to control her bicycle. Twenty feet from the crowd she fell off and burst into catastrophic tears. Some of the women from the group gathered around her and helped her up. "Tell him I am so sorry. I'm so sorry." Hugo felt the man's arm authoritatively and pronounced him fit, but I saw his face and knew he was in pain. One of them spoke to me in English. "You are ladies?" They seemed bemused by the men's clothing. Were they Gypsies? Hugo gave them money and they went on. Zoë calmed down. The sun came out from behind a cloud.

And now I want to try to remember Zoë's questions and his answers. I said she asked a thousand questions, but what? For example one late afternoon on the doorstep at Holland Street.

"See you tomorrow," said Zoë, taking his hand. We were saying good-bye in the doorway after a day of rambling around the city together. Susannah had called us to tea. He had to go off to a meeting.

"Insha'Allah," he said, bending to kiss the top of her head.

"What does that mean?"

"If God is willing."

"What?" She pulled on his hand, didn't want him to go. "Wait. What does that mean?"

"Everything we do or plan or think depends on God's will," he said, seriously, turning back to her, looking directly at her.

"Everything?"

"Yes." He smiled. I was totally excluded from this exchange and I watched as though hypnotized.

"Why?"

"This is God's world."

"God controls everything?" He nodded. She thought for a moment, not letting go. "So if God controls everything, God is bad."

"Why do you say that?"

"Because if He was good, He wouldn't let all these bad things happen." She waved her arm to include the terrible poverty we'd seen that day down by the river, her parents' death perhaps, the war in Africa. He smiled, sadly I thought, and shook his head.

She tssked and shook her head hard, thinking, holding him, not letting go. "What is God?"

"God is the Divine in everything."

"What is divine?"

"God in everything."

"Is God in trees?"

"Yes."

"Is God in trees that are cut down."

"Well," he paused a moment, "yes."

"So you are God?"

"Yes."

"I am God?"

"Yes."

"She's God?" Zoë didn't look at me, just tipped her head back a bit towards where I was standing dumbfounded behind them.

"Yes, of course."

The Modern Age

"So God makes bad things happen?"

"Well yes."

"Why?"

"Well," He paused, caught my eye for a second. "Because we have free will. We have to be allowed to choose to do bad things."

"Why?"

"I don't know, sweetheart."

"Stupid," she said and marched past him into the dim house where tea was waiting.

He took my hand for a moment, said, "See you tomorrow," and was gone, swinging down the street.

A child's questions. A child who has had a sweet day and doesn't want the sweetness to end so asks tiresome childish questions. And he answered seriously, the best he could I suppose, and still his answers were no answers. The questions stand.

Why do people suffer? Why did Zoë suffer? I believe now even her beauty was suffering to her. What cruel God sets us up to test our patience and forbearance? Is that what suffering is for? How can God be both All Good and All Powerful?

Oh well. I just wear myself out with this kind of thing.

And I have my own questions. Or question, the question that keeps coming back no matter how I keep it at bay: Why did Hugo leave me?

Why? We had so much fun together in those spring days. He got boots the right size, his big hands on my small

The Modern Age

feet measuring. We went to concerts, Sir Charles Perry giving one of his large oratorios. By 1900, the Impressionists were accepted in London and we went to a show. We went about on the streets looking at everything. That year, girls wore buttons with photographs of the Boer War Generals on them: Lord Roberts, Butler, Kitchener, White. We saw Rupert Brooke with bare legs in a play. We talked about going to the Paris Universal Exhibition to see Xray photography and Wireless Telegraphy. The Fair was run by electricity and you could tour the site on an electrically powered moving platform with three tiers, each rolling at different speeds. The sculptor, August Rodin was displayed in a separate pavilion. Rebecca West said of this time, "Everything looked like it was going to get better quite quickly," and so it seemed. But we didn't make it to the fair

Hugo lived in a Studio facing east for the morning sun. Right outside the window, lime trees burst into green bud. He said the sumac turned brilliant red in the fall but he was gone from my life before fall came round again. Inside his flat he had many wonderful things from his travels. Peruvian pots and Javanese puppets glowed soft brown on low tables. African fetishes leered from the mantelpiece and Tibetan paintings leaned against the walls. There wasn't enough space on the bookshelves for the stacks of books and manuscript pages so these were here and there around the room.

I risked a great deal to meet him there at his rooms. I risked my reputation, which apparently had some value in those days. I risked my life, should I get pregnant. I risked syphilis, that horrible disease of lesions, tumours, and lunacy. One of the literary sub-genres of the time was novels by women writers about men who brought their wives syphilis. It was not funny. I risked Uncle Cornelius' wrath, no small thing.

When I arrived the first time, the door was open; he called for me to come in. He was playing the piano and whistling a song.

The man had a gift for friendship. There was often someone there when I arrived. Different kinds of people, sometimes older men who talked with him about exploration and religion. Once or twice another woman, older, married perhaps, who came with books and left with other books. Once I was introduced and had tea with an Arab man in a striped robe. He and Hugo spoke a foreign language and Hugo translated the odd bit. What he translated was perfectly mundane but I was sure what he didn't translate must have been quite interesting.

Zoë was my accomplice in arranging these illicit meetings. The Tate Gallery had opened three years before. I would take Zoë there or to the National Gallery or the National Portrait Gallery. I then took the Underground to Hugo's, spent my afternoons, and rushed back on the Underground to collect Zoë at whatever Art Gallery she was at. It amused me to think how the Underground, this wonder of the modern age, was whisking me and others like me to afternoon assignations. It made sin so easy. I spent my afternoons like a poor person who has been given a sudden gift of money, that is with great profligacy.

Zoë was also pleased with this arrangement. She loved to look at paintings and would not be rushed from one to another. One afternoon she saw Aunt Lavender at the gallery. She tried to hide but Lavender saw her and quizzed her about who she was with and tried to arrange a tea party in the café. Zoë convinced her that I was mesmerized by the Turners in another room and we had to be somewhere very soon. She was ten. Such a smart girl. Zoë Zoë, how I miss you even now.

But I've been indulging myself, letting myself run on here about Hugo and myself. Zoë is never out of my mind, but I don't seem to be able to write about her properly. I feel like a cowboy who knows every sign of the sky and the clouds and the winds and can only say, "Looks like rain." All that experience and knowledge and so inarticulate.

I watched Zoë at the Portrait Gallery one late afternoon

when the Underground had flung me back to her early. She was looking at the paintings of kings and walking backwards and forwards squinting, until a strange male face became only colour and brushstrokes. Her blouse was untucked and her hat off and hanging from her hand. On the way home she told me that there had been indigo, orange madder, cerise, and plum in the beard. She loved the names of colours and studied them. I had no way of knowing if she was right or not, but she was happy telling me about her precious colours.

But there was something wrong with Zoë. I didn't focus on it. I didn't do anything about it. I didn't listen to my own inner knowledge. I regret.

SEVEN

Another sleepless night, three hours staring out the window into the wet darkness shining in the street light, and it seems I must totally tell the Hugo part of the story, with no omissions. Why this is I cannot say.

Up to this point, these were the parts of my body he had touched: my hands, the inside of my arms, my feet (measuring them for boots), my lips, the back of my head, my shoulders, my back (through many layers of clothing), my cheeks, my eyes, and my nose. The parts of his body that I had touched

The Modern Age

were: his hands, his lips, his springy hair, his shoulders and part of his back through clothes, the back of his neck, and his throat.

It was not enough. I wanted to be touched everywhere. When I wore the men's pants and the rough tweed rubbed on the inside of my thighs I wanted his hands and kisses to smooth the skin better. I wanted my breasts and my stomach and the small of my back to feel his brushing touch. I wanted to touch all of him. Through his clothing I could see the shadow of muscles in his arms and legs. I wanted to trace them with my fingers. I wanted to see where the veins went and how they curled up his arm. I wanted to feel the whole weight of him on my small body.

The fourth time I went to his rooms, he wasn't there. He'd left a note. Back in a few minutes. My light boots were wet from cutting across the park. I took them off. I thought about taking off all my clothes and sitting on the sofa to wait. I took off my stockings and put them across the shoes by the door. I was abandoned, beyond theology, beyond shame, beyond thought. I sat for a moment with my heart pounding, determined to "give myself to him". I got up and paced. I picked a Peruvian statue off the mantel but my hands shook. I put it back. I opened a door. It was his bedroom. I crossed in, thinking: I have crossed a threshold. I closed my eyes and paced the outside of the room, touching flocked walls with my fingertips. I came to his closet and walked into the wall of dark suits. I buried my face in the wool and inhaled his smell. I ran my hands along the coats and into some of the pockets. This is how he found me, barefoot in his cupboard.

I turned to greet him, my back against his suit coats. Hugo filled the room, then came to me, his coat rough and wet. My cheek brushed his shoulder. There were huge drops of water in his hair, the smell of wet wool and his manly smell.

"Yes?" he said.

"Yes."

The Modern Age

He made love to me nicely, slowly. He was interested in me. I was able to see all that I wanted to see and he saw all he wanted to see too. So strange how a man and a woman fit together so nicely when they want to. When we came to, it was strangely still afternoon, with time to dress and go and get Zoë.

Birth control? I don't think so. He said he would be careful and I suppose he was. I was lucky. Funny to think now that Aunt Lavender went her whole life without knowing anything about the way that men and women come together. And Zoë later, as a pregnant woman, was outraged at the Double Standard. Men could have sexual intercourse with whom they pleased, regardless of the consequences to the family.

That day I dressed again: a burgundy devore shawl over a lemon yellow lawn blouse and a dark wool skirt. I remember every detail. My stockings and boots still damp.

My mouse heart jumped to his hands and stayed and wanted to stay forever.

If I had waited to make love to him, would Hugo have married me and honoured the contract? When he first left, I was very angry and ashamed and thought that I should never have slept with him. Now I think we might have continued a bit longer as half-lovers, almost lovers, in that intense haze of sexual heat, but I think now that he still would have left. He was strange. We only had a half dozen times together there in his rooms.

Why did Hugo leave? That was never answered. What if we had married and then he had gone to fight at the Marne and been killed. I would have been a widow instead of a spinster. At least I would have had those years with him. How would that have been? Zoë came back to Canada in 1914, playing the role of widow, totally believable, pregnant in black, weeping and red-eyed.

But sorrow is a bruise on my heart, which will never heal now.

Longing is a sorrow that we all live with forever. We are separated from our love, from our true selves, from our completeness, our God.

I have received honours, decorations, ribbons, medals, badges, certificates, an honourary doctorate. I am stoic, blasé, unmoved. From the Bureau of Recognition, they should issue an honourary doctorate for getting through a bad day. For walking the dog.

I shall excise all this before I let anyone see it.

EIGHT

It was only May when he announced he was leaving, lilac time. We sat in wicker chairs under the darkest of the purple lilacs, almost fainting with lilac scent. Three chairs, morning coffee. The smell and the feeling of bliss come back to me vividly even now. Then he told me, he told me, he was breaking off the engagement. He told me.

"Mary-Margaret I have something to say," taking my hand in his and saying it. "I am afraid I have to break off our engagement." And turned to Zoë, before I could speak, and ever so gently said he was leaving, going away for a long trip.

We sat there a moment, shocked, silent in the lilac scent, then Zoë did what I wanted to do, flung herself on his lap in wild tears. She loved him too. I had my period; I knew I

The Modern Age

wasn't pregnant and couldn't hold him in that way. In some strange part of my mind I believe he knew too. I don't understand why he broke it off. He said he was sorry three times before he left. He didn't try to explain. I didn't ask any questions. I was passive, in shock. He didn't try to say that it was no life for me to be waiting for him. We both knew I would have waited. He had some kind of inner certainty; he'd received some kind of message I believe. He was very sorry. He did love me. I know that. I still don't understand. But it was done in such a way that it had to be accepted.

But before I could accept, I became ill. On May 17, 1900 the siege of Mafeking was over. The news came that Baden-Powell had held out long enough and the British forces had finally arrived to relieve them from the terrible Boers. There was joy in the streets. I was caught out in the wild celebration. I was wandering alone, heartsick, the afternoon of the day after he told me, and was jostled by a shrieking, whistling crowd. Grotesques capered with false noses, men and girls danced together with penny whistles. An old lady cackled and tickled my face with a long feather. Then someone lit firecrackers off right under my feet. By the time I got back to Holland Street I was desperate, gasping for air, and very sick. The world went dim and distant. My throat was swollen shut. My chest hurt to move at all. Coughing. Fever.

I have not been able to work on this for a week.

The nephew came, together with his wife, an ominous sign, to talk to me AGAIN about possibly Going In A Home. They mean well but I have not been answering the phone for a week and have had a locksmith in to change the locks. My independence is the one thing I have that is mine; it is my daughter, my son, mine own thing. Aside from the dog. I cherish my independence. I do not take it for granted, various degrees of debility notwithstanding.

He was prodded by his wife, a lovely girl, I just know it. When I'm angry, I get very quiet, as that boy should know by now. Angry at myself, angry at them. So angry I've just been sitting and pacing and sitting since the locksmith left. I can hardly eat and I feel myself getting weaker. But I've roused myself and had a good feed of tuna fish to try to finish this.

I've always been a flinger. I would fling myself into a chair, fling a scarf around my neck. Finally the other day I flung Morgan and wife out. Fortunately they are relatively civilized and would not dream of using force against me but I am acutely aware of how small I am, of how I have in fact shrunk, and I started small. He hugged me. I am shrunk in his arms.

Those manly men. It brings back all those ugly males at medical college mocking me every single day I was there. And Uncle Cornelius with his smirk, his hands behind his back, rocking on his toes, the life of the party, charming us, showing Zoë how to throw grapes up and catch them in her mouth. "This is how Queen Victoria eats grapes."

It's strange to feel angry again after all this time as if the poison had been sealed in the cells and this provocation broke the seals and released it into the blood. And this morning I woke up with a memory, which I had entirely lost, which seems to have been released along with this anger towards Morgan. Now I'm not angry at my nephew at all any more. I'm sure we can work it out. But it's as if some primitive part of myself was awakened by his paternalism and fought back. And now I remember what Cornelius did after Hugo said he was leaving and before I got sick. How strange that I could have forgotten this so completely.

Now it comes back to me in jumpy bits: how I spent a sleepless, dry-eyed night after Hugo made his gentle announcement, the feel of his final handshake on my hand. Gone. How I went the next morning to Uncle Cornelius's study and begged him to send me to medical school, to help me. How he frowned and shook his head. The second time of asking.

The Modern Age

How at tea he took ten-year-old Zoë between his legs with his arms across her smocked chest and made fun of me and my unwomanly ambitions. How Zoë was forced to laugh a hollow sound from that caged chest. How Susannah sided with him, laughed and betrayed her principles.

And suddenly another memory flickers to consciousness: Susannah old, in the middle of the Second World War, long after Cornelius was gone, with long white hair which I would comb and pin up for her. Thin hair, long and flat, hard to pin up, silky like corn silk but white. She whimpered when I dressed her after her stroke. The Old sacrifice their modesty when they need to be taken care of, but not their sense of shame. I don't think of myself as old, but now I am. Now I am The Old and not ready to sacrifice my privacy, my independence, no matter what Morgan and his busy wife-lady say.

Susannah. When she was young she must have been attracted to the freewheeling entertainer in Cornelius. Everything else she did in a methodical rational way, but must have been swept up in the imperative to get married and unsure of whether anyone else would ever want her. She would never say so, but perhaps she later wondered if she would have been better to remain single. But she did love him. After the stroke, years after he killed himself, she asked for him. He's dead, Auntie, I would say. "Oh so they tell me." She was not interested in rank or title. In some ways she was the most self-confident woman I have ever known, in other ways the least. Authority didn't impress her. Mostly she rolled her eyes at Cornelius's pronouncements. And I would have said that normally she operated independently of him, was her own woman. But that May afternoon, at tea in the garden, with Zoë caught between his legs facing out, his hands across her white dress, his chin resting on her glossy dark hair, joking at my desire to make a life of my own, Susannah crossed over to his side, laughed at me, let me go. I don't know whether they knew that Hugo had dropped me at that point. Zoë did.

The Modern Age

It was always assumed that Cornelius was playing devil's advocate with a twinkle in his eye and that he also knew and believed it was right that women should vote and that their participation in the political system would provide a sort of moral impetus to improve everything everywhere. Now I wonder. His arguments, made in a merry jousting fashion, now seem to me the solid bedrock of belief underpinning Men's Power, which continues to hold sway unabated despite women's suffrage and women such as myself entering the workforce. Women would be emotional and make bad decisions. He joked about how I would be in surgery and it would be "that time" and I would be in tears and my patient dead while I was weeping. Women were unable to see the big picture. The joke was something about worrying about what the patient was wearing while he was dying of syphilis. I don't want even to start dealing with these ideas, just that I now see more clearly, or know more deeply, what I was up against. I am very angry. Cornelius seemed fun and jolly and easy-going and I was so surprised that, when he told me that I could not go to medical school, I could not go. His word was law. He controlled the money and there was a reason for that and there would be no money provided.

And then it must have been the next day that I got caught in the Mafeking craziness and then I was sick.

I was in a fever for a long time and had vivid hallucinations. Dreaming of traveling, walking in the Andes, walking where the air is thin, my bones not aching, the sky blue, llamas bleating, and the stars at night. Crying yellow onion tears.

Climbing. I was always climbing in those hallucinations. Climbing waterfalls, trees, fences, jumping from a shed roof onto compost. Compost hot on the bare feet. Jumping and climbing up again, jumping and climbing. Hiding too, hiding in the hazelnut thicket, in the bamboo thicket. Searching in the woods for Hugo.

It seemed so obvious that I would die. Everyone else had died. I felt that I would die. They say, "She lay inches from death," and truly that's how it felt, that I lay at the edge of whatever death is, a pit, a cliff, a melting. I wanted to die. When they say, "She died of heartbreak," I believe that can happen, because I lay in that bed, my head hot and all of me in pain and I wanted to die.

Now I cling to this brittle life so hard my fingers hurt. It seems so strange that then I was ready to go, could easily have slipped away. Would have missed so much.

After all these deaths, my illness and the devastation of realizing that Hugo was not going to marry me, or make love to me any more (I would have settled for that), I was barely alive. The illness was a time of fever, dark red shifting shapes, distant worried voices, a sense of Zoë nearby, pain, coughing.

Zoë told me later that she prayed for me to live and I think that's what I remember from that time, a sense of darkness with a fierce Zoë spirit near my ear whispering. Then, I did not think of that as healing. I was grateful for her presence for I loved her always, but I believed that the doctors made me better with their medicine and that belief added to my sleeping desire to be a doctor.

Lying in bed after that illness, floating in the clear light of simply being alive, I saw that I would never marry, some women didn't, and it was acceptable to me. Hugo was the love of my life and he was gone. Later of course when the War cut through a generation of young men, not marrying was not as unusual, not as shameful. I saw in that clear light that I would not marry and I would become a doctor and dedicate myself to the world, to assisting at the birth of modernism.

No doubt that sounds quaint and naive now after two wars and the holocaust and all that went with it. But disease was almost over. Typhoid and cholera epidemics were almost a thing of the past due to improved sanitation and water. Vaccinations were coming in for smallpox. Syphilis remained a nasty problem but there were reform movements geared at changing men's behavior so that innocent women would not be harmed and the sexes could be on a more equal footing sexually. I didn't know it at the time but salvarsan, the arsenic treatment for syphilis, was just a few years away. The knowledge that something could be done was in the air. And of course then we did not have any idea about antibiotics.

While I lay there, near death, they tried at first to keep Zoë away. But she came in. She had to sneak at first because they did not want her near me, for fear she would get sick, or because they thought she would bother me. But she was very strong and came anyway. She bullied the servants and stood by my bed arguing with me in her fierce whisper. I don't think I actually spoke but in my mind I argued stubbornly with her and she won.

"What if you only get one chance," she rasped. "You get one body, one chance to be alive in this world. And you want to go and die before you've found out anything?" She said all the things I would have said to her if I had known she wanted to hurl herself in the river: "You'll just have to come back and do it all again. Come on Em that's stupid."

Where was I when she was on the other side of the argument?

Everyone died. My mother, my father, my brother, Kate, and then worst of all Zoë. I was helpless each time. Why so upset about Zoë? Why so obsessed? We all die. Everyone dies. Everyone has a list of his or her dead. What happened when each one died? How we weigh the weight of a soul passing from the earth. How the curtains blew out when my mother died. How there was silence when my father died. How the day shone and sparkled the day George and Kate died. And the one I draw near and draw away from. Zoë died. Where was I? Darkness surrounds my memory. Her child, Morgan, was home with the nurse. I must have been at work, in my comfortable office with its polished desk and glass front cases, or at the hospital. There was no sign, no word. Darkness. Her

The Modern Age

dying words, unknown. Her dying wish, unspoken. How could I have prevented this death, as I seem to think? How did I cause it? Surely I am not so God-like. Surely I do not have so much power. Hindoo -- if she was destined to die that way at that time? The seed of her death was contained in her birth. Her mother Kate drinking and drunk sometimes, did that have some effect? Her death is a whirlpool that pulls me down into it, my head caught underwater, blackness with red at the edges like rage, jams me up against logs and holds me there breathless.

Now I am dying, this I know. My seed of death is about to burst into bloom, just this one thing to settle before I go. But what if it was time to go but you were blocked, kept from continuing, but it was time? What if you know it is not time but swept away by it anyhow, helpless to stop it? I know it is almost my time. Penny has written that she has found letters addressed to me in Susannah's things and is bringing them when she comes home. Letters addressed to me but unopened. I suppose I shall have to at least stay alive to see what that is all about. And I find I am as avid as a greedy child to know.

That's what Morgan and his wife meant coming to me together to try to get me into a Home. They know it is my time and they want to hire someone else to be the one to find my body because they are afraid to find me dead. I saw it often at the hospital; people told me they were afraid of Grandma, or their Mama being so sick and dying. But it is nothing, not fearful, just there and then not. I didn't realize this when Morgan was here, I should have told him. The curtains bell out, the life is gone. I like that expression "gone to spirit". Perhaps that's all it is.

I wish I had the fortitude to tell Morgan he's afraid, but we never talked like that. Now I write without restraint, knowing someone will read this soon, soon enough, and by then I will be gone.

I am afraid. I am not afraid. I believe nothing. I believe everything. I don't know. In one fairy tale, my mother stands radiant in heaven, arms outstretched, exactly the age she was when she died. I come into her arms and I am a child of five forever. But then I must turn and greet my nephew that way, somehow the exact age he expects me to be.

That summer, summer of 1900, disappeared, lost to fever, and then there was the long light of autumn shining through yellow leaves. Being alive, not being dead: Zoë and I sitting on the floor eating from plates. Now if only I could kiss her lovely freckled face.

I was near death, and then gradually getting better for about ten weeks. When I was finally well enough to join family life again, but not fully better, Cornelius said to me in a gentle voice, "This illness proves I am right about this foolish medical school idea. Women are certainly too fragile to undergo the rigours of hard academic training and understanding of the human body. We will hear no more about that." Then he looked around to Susannah and gave her a firm nod as if punctuating the end of that discussion and included Zoë in the gesture for good measure. Then, out of guilt I suppose, he had a greenhouse built for me.

NINE

What do you suppose Penny is bringing me? Letters she said, unopened. Why is she so enigmatic? Perhaps they're letters from whoever was Zoë's lover, Morgan's father. Perhaps Penny will solve that mystery finally. She asked me about it before she left, curious, wanting to do research, but Zoë never told me anything. One time I asked Zoë outright, when she was pregnant. I said to myself it was a medical matter and I needed to know. I spoke standing, white-coated, stethoscope in hand. Zoë looked at me and said, "There was a little girl, who had a little curl, right in the middle of her forehead. When she was good, she was very very good, and when she was bad, she was horrid." Horrid. Horrid.

It would be nice to have all the mysteries solved before I go, to have them all neatly filed away. Who was Zoë's lover? Why Hugo left me? How I managed at all when he did? I suppose I have to give Cornelius some credit. He forced me outside again, out into the world. I might have simply given up. I was that close. Cornelius and the greenhouse.

Then, Autumn 1900, Cornelius bustled around, a busy sack of flesh, whispering, droning, buzzing, conspiratorial with Susannah and Zoë, and mysterious with workmen, not telling me, and I too sick to care. I didn't realize the bustle even pertained to me until a beautiful cold day in October, with frost dazzling on the grass, my heart cold to it. Zoë took me into the garden. The grapes shone and smelled sweet, as if they might be edible, though Susannah insisted they never were. This family's grapes will always will always taste bitter in the end even if starting sweet, end bitter. Red leaves glowed by the fence, evangelizing: stay alive stay alive. Zoë held me by the hand. Zoë's hand sent the same leaf message, smaller than mine but her soul bigger. Cornelius and Susannah arrived by the library door, wavering through glass, grownups. Zoë pulled out a long paisley scarf, made me bend down to her and wrapped it round my eyes. In darkness. Outside myself were wavering grownups, Zoë's hand. They led me out into the garden, down the stone steps, past the gazebo - I could see the wooden posts out the bottom of the scarf - and to the back where the hazel thicket had been. Zoë removed the blindfold with a flourish and there it was, shining in the slanting light -- a greenhouse for me. Oh beauty, glass shining shining all around slowly circling glass and warmth.

I'd never wanted a greenhouse. I'd never shown any interest in greenhouses or gardening. But Cornelius, in his particular genius, decided it was just what the doctor ordered. He led us all around the outside and then the inside, showing me the gravel floor for holding humidity, a fan for providing the breezes that some plants need, the canvas shades on rollers that could be pulled down when the sun was too hot, tanks under the stages to gather rainwater for the plants, and a pump so the water level could be raised in dry weather. "Just what the doctor ordered," he said.

For all I know it was just what my doctor had ordered. In those days, people who had tuberculosis were told to work in greenhouses. The warm humid air was said to be good for them. I didn't have tuberculosis but God knows I needed something because I was flattened. They never could say what it was, or give my illness a name. Maybe it was the influenza that hit the world eighteen years later. I was working in Vancouver then and almost died of exhaustion but never got the flu.

Ten weeks since I'd been out on the street on Mafeking Day. About seven weeks of acute illness and three weeks of dully sitting and aching with tiredness, not able even to read. Zoë said all the sparkle had gone out of me. Cornelius was right I suppose, much as I still hate to give him anything: that greenhouse did bring me back to life. I spent hours there, certainly the hours Zoë was in school, for while I was sick they'd decided to educate her a bit more regularly and sent her off to Miss Bishop's, a school for young ladies. Anyway I didn't have the childish energy to play with her anymore. That had been knocked right out of me. At first I had only enough energy to walk down to the glass house and sit in the corner in the threadbare red plush chair from the library that Susannah had donated. I wasn't sure I would ever be better. Sometimes I almost cried sitting there, though never outwardly.

I started to work with plants. I puttered. Jim, the old gardener, helped me at first then left me on my own. I repotted houseplants that Susannah had acquired and then ignored over the years. I nursed a philodendron back to life. It wasn't much. The glass house was the right size for me, ten feet long by eight feet wide with glass shelves and a wooden countertop. Standing at the counter, I looked out across the garden to the house and could see people coming and going, Susannah wistful at the library window, the cook sitting down for a cigarette outside the kitchen door, the gardener working slowly around the beds. It gave a pleasant distance from that house. I spent long hours opening and closing panels trying to figure out how to regulate the temperature. It was not a hot house or "stove" as I learned to call them, but a glass house, mostly heated by the sun but with a small wood stove.

Often I grew tired of gardening. I felt weak for a long time. Then, I sat in a corner of the warm glass house. Sometimes I read, sometimes I dozed, and sometimes I just sat. Now I see that this was a time of gathering. This was a time when, being a rejected woman and then so sick, I had been pretty much purged of all that I had been, or had hoped for myself, and I was left empty. Slowly, working in the glass house, something of what I might be began to fill me up. I suppose it is not so strange that it was not really different than what I had said I wanted before. It was rather that I began to see that I actually could do what I had idly said I would. I just didn't know how. I gradually became more determined somehow to go to medical school. I was calmer.

After my strength began to come back, I started reading again to prepare for entrance examinations. I worked slowly through the material, the Greek and Latin and anatomy. My mind seemed clearer after my illness, washed clean of the idea that Hugo would ever come back to me. Susannah and Zoë knew what I was doing. We had a tacit agreement not to speak to Cornelius about it.

The orchids arrived on my birthday in November. There was no card but it was obvious from whom they came. The gift gave the family the impression that we were still engaged. Indeed confirmed that we were, because otherwise it would be quite wrong to accept it. But we had no idea what the big parcel was worth. Anyway, I at least, knew it was over between us. Inside the wooden crate was a dried up mass of almost dead plant material, and under that, an oilskin pouch, wrapped tightly with twine. Inside the pouch was a wad of paper torn from a journal with descriptions written in green ink of conditions where the plants had been taken. I looked through these papers closely, first just to try to figure out where he was. Night temperatures, wind, rainfall, humidity, elevation were all carefully recorded but it could have been anywhere. The crate had been sent from Southampton so that was no clue. I understood that the place where the orchids had been taken was a secret and would remain a secret because of the extremely competitive nature of orchid hunting. Actually the days of the fierce orchid hunters were long over, maybe fifty years earlier, but Hugo, bless him, had found something special.

Questions I had then and never got answered:

Did he know that it was my birthday and send it for that?

Did he know I'd been ill?

Did he know that I had a glass house where I could nurture these plants?

I suppose these questions go with me to the incinerator. Certainly no one answered them at the time. One clue was the memory of the gift he had given me when I was fifteen, a week before I left to return to Montreal, a small painting of a Chinese orchid, very pale and yet intense with open lips, as though the flower was panting, pale purple and green with folds of deepest rose. The painting was left behind when my brother died and Zoë and I were shipped out. I had to leave it because I was not in charge. I was mowed down. Anyway it disappeared, much to my regret.

In Chinese, orchids are called lan; they symbolize the sweetness of friendship. Hugo sent a card with the painting with a poem written out in his hand:

From the Shih Ching Book of Poems, edited by Confucius:

The Modern Age

"Shin and Yu are full of water now,
For spring has come to melt the snow,
And men and women of the state wear lan now,
She says to him, There let us go
To see the places. He says: No,
For I have seen the places years ago.
She says again: There let us go;
There is a place beyond the river Yu
Where we can our love do."

When I was fifteen, almost sixteen, we did not our love do.

I had to borrow a hammer from Jim the gardener, and he helped me open the muddy crate on the black and white tiles of the kitchen floor. I had bouts of weakness that came on me suddenly and I moved slowly as if my body was something fragile. I ended up sitting on a chair while he pulled back the top slats. Bits of damp tropical soil fell out. Zoë watched avidly.

We unpacked the box and found these wretched bits of plant. "What am I supposed to do with these?" I knew they were orchids because he had talked so much about them, about struggle and thrill. I knew that they needed some kind of special care because he'd told me, with scorn, how British growers were too stupid to keep orchids alive. I was angry. I didn't want his orchids. I didn't want this challenge. I told Jim to put the crate in the greenhouse and just leave it.

I meant to just leave it and I did not sleep well, with unpleasant feverish dreams, but I went out into the city the next morning as soon as Zoë went to school and got a copy of The Orchid Growers Manual. It was the first time I had been out since my illness and I wasn't really strong enough. It was a wretched November day with freezing rain and wind. I wasn't wearing boots; my feet got wet. When I got home I went straight to my room, stripped out of my wet things, and lay on the bed with the book under the pillow. It was too much. I resolved that I wouldn't do it. When they called for luncheon I didn't get up and Susannah came herself to see if I had collapsed again. I begged off lunch though I was actually hungry. The room tilted and billowed. I felt that I might be sick for the rest of my life. Sick, sickly, dying and shrouded in convention. I slept for a while and had strange dreams again. When I woke up something had shifted.

Something in me laughed at the idea of making those orchids live. Women weren't supposed to own orchids. The shapes of the flowers were considered too sexually suggestive. But the Queen herself was a passionate orchid fancier and appointed a Royal Orchid Grower. For her Golden Jubilee, he made an orchid bouquet seven feet high and five feet wide. Wicked orchids with their sexual flowers. Orchids were at various times considered: Carnivorous, Poisonous, Wicked, Mysterious, and Seductive. Of course I felt I could never live up to them.

It was unladylike to be interested in orchids. But suddenly I was interested. I wanted to see what kind of flowers he'd sent me. I wanted to know what colour they would be when I woke up in the morning and what colour they would be in evening light. So I got up the next morning and went out to the greenhouse with my new book and stayed there all day, reading and arranging bits of plant in pots with charcoal and soil and potshards and moss.

Following the instructions in the book, I sponged over every leaf and bulb and cut away bits of decayed plant with a sharp knife. Sometimes now out walking, especially in Stanley Park in the fall, I catch a whiff of something that reminds me of the smell that filled the room as I cut carefully at the bulbs. I laid the bits of root on dry moss shaded from the sun and gave a little water, light, and heat. It was like treating a feeble patient who has just come out of the tunnel of sickness. Like me.

Susannah came out twice that day to scold me for overdoing it. Zoë came to scold me when she came home from school, and stayed to watch and then to sketch the strange roots reaching out from the bulbs. From then on I spent all day, every day, in the greenhouse for almost three years. Zoë was there often, drawing and painting the flowers.

Confucius wrote about orchids in the fifth century before Christ, and Theophratus in the third century B.C. Orchids were in use in China for medical purposes three thousand years ago and were listed in Dioscorides in the Materia Medica in the First Century AD. In the nineteenth century after Christ, Europeans discovered orchids. In 1818, a man named William Cattley was unpacking some plants from Brazil, and decided to try to grow the weird little bulbs that had been used as packing material. The result was Cattleya labiata, the Queen of Flowers. Collecting orchids of the world became a mania of the rich and adventurous of Europe.

Hugo told orchid hunting tales at dinner and to learned societies in London and Cambridge. Though the great age of orchid collection was over, people like Hugo who still collected had become furtive in their business. Orchid collectors were bold adventurous young men, attacked by rain, snakes, animals, insects, disease, rapids, floods, natives, and other orchid hunters. Orchid hunting was a life of secrecy, hiding, and competition. One story Hugo told was about how his sampan caught fire. "The lines of my raft were cut and a whole boatload of orchids stolen." A European nursery offered 10,000 pounds for the rediscovery of Pahiopedilum fairieanum. Collectors had picked every known specimen of the Fairy orchid. (It eventually reappeared in cultivation). It was not unusual to pay 17 pounds for a single orchid at auction in London or Liverpool. Hugo said that one rare specimen went for 700 pounds.

In 1894, before I met him, when he was only twenty, Hugo was one of twenty collectors sent by Messrs Sanders into the jungles of Brazil, Columbia, Peru, Ecuador, Mexico, Madagascar, New Guinea, India, Burma, and the Straits Settlements. They stripped whole areas of trees to gather the epiphytic orchids from upper branches. The areas where Miltonia vexillania were found were cleared as if by forest fires. In one search for Odontoglossum crispum in Columbia, they collected ten thousand plants; four thousand trees were felled. One of the collectors sent thirty boxes of orchids home and wrote: "They are nearly extinguished in this spot and this will surely be the last season. All along the Rio Daqua there are no plants left." So Hugo told us at dinner with no trace of regret.

By the turn of the century the mania was mostly over, only a few were still making money collecting orchids.

Orchids are supposed to stand for refinement, friendship, perfection, numerous progeny, all things feminine, noble, and elegant. So perhaps it is best that I left them behind when I ran away, or if I hadn't, I might have turned out differently. Certainly I am not refined. I have had friends but am alone now and have attended many funerals. I am far from perfect, have no progeny, have taken up the most unfeminine of trades, and I am certainly not noble or elegant. But it turned out that cultivating orchids was something I was good at. Mainly it involved understanding the needs of the flowers and carefully meeting them. And Hugo had given me in that crate something really special.

The orchid Hugo sent me, which I grew in my little greenhouse in London was, like the first orchids that came to England, also a Cattleya, C. amerilia, a "lost orchid", that is an orchid that had been ravaged from its wild habitat, killed off in too hot glass houses in England and Belgium, and unknown to collectors for almost fifty years. That's why it was so special. Hugo wouldn't say where he found it. About a year after he sent the box of bulbs, he wrote me a letter from Cornwall again, a letter friendly but distant, and I wrote back to the address I'd had before and tried to get him to tell me where the orchid came from. He didn't write again except for the few impersonal postcards that came from time to time. By then I'd had the orchid identified and knew what I had and that I could make a great deal of money from it.

He didn't even say what continent, though Cattleyas generally grew in the northern part of South America and up through Central America. The original Cattleya amerilia plants were collected from moist rocks along streams in ravines in Costa Rica.

There are at least sixty species of Cattleya. Most are lythophytic, that is they grow on rock, but this one was epiphytic, growing in the tops of trees. I hung them from wires on slatted open baskets or pieces of bark. The orchid was sympodial, many stems joined by a rhizome. The leaves were thick and fleshy, the inflorescence terminal, the flowers several, the pseudobulbs, where the plants store food and water, obovoid-clavate (long and oval) up to 12 inches high. The plants grew twenty-two inches high and the flowers five inches across. It had the typical Cattleya labellum, with a large ornate stalkless flower. The side lobes were folding and rather tube shaped. It had a tall upright dorsal sepal, bright green. And aerial roots. That is the technical description. The aerial roots were palest green and twisted in a pleasing way, forming a hanging frieze against the light. I would look and look, never getting enough of the fleshy bright leaves, bending slightly at the top, the thick bulbs bursting with life. Zoë drew them and painted them.

Then my orchids bloomed. Many orchids have funny faces, or look like something else, like a humming bird, a lady's purse, or an insect. But this one looked only like itself, an abstract version of itself. The flower was lavender, a sort of dim subtle purple-blue, with thin, barely perceptible, red stripes along the lip ending in a red-striped fringe, like the fringe on a shawl. "Praemorse" said the man on the phone from Kew Gardens whom I consulted to identify it. He came out the very day I called for a look through thick glasses, and was responsible for spreading the word among orchid fanciers and would-be fanciers that I had something really special. The inside of the orchid's throat was bright red. It was very beautiful in a strange way, if I haven't conveyed that, and it had a sweet lemony scent.

The note enclosed in the crate, written in green ink in Hugo's hand, said it grew on the higher branches of trees in a shady but bright ravine near a stream with many ferns, bromeliads, and mosses nearby. And not far from ocean breezes. The expert took one look and said Jamaica, which made sense because that was the last place I heard from Hugo, before he sent them. One of his cryptic but energetic postcards, which I received occasionally until I left for Canada: "Gully beans and fish soup. Green light." He would never confirm that the orchid was from Jamaica.

I learned to propagate the orchid by dividing the root bound plant. Cut it apart and break it. After a while I discovered it grew better on pieces of bark than in pots. Soon I had many orchid babies.

For ocean breezes I gave it the fan that Cornelius had provided. The book said Brazilian orchids need a cooler and less moist atmosphere. 60 degrees at night and 65-70 during the day. I assumed it was a Brazilian-type orchid and my assumption seemed to work. The orchids rested from November to mid February. I followed the instructions to lower the temperature and withhold water, giving only enough to keep the plants from shriveling. They did some growing but I kept the shoots dry and the house warm.

While the plants rested, I washed every pane of glass inside and outside, also the wood and brickwork. Cleanliness is necessary for good results, said the book. I moved the plants around until they seemed to like a spot. I took notes. In the May to August growing season, I increased the house temperature from 65 to 70 up to 85 degrees by day. I noticed that I seemed to have more energy.

The first time someone called for one of my orchids I was called to the phone and held it standing dazzled in evening sun in the polished hallway of the big house. A bright red piece of fabric over the back of a chair threw up a red shadow on the wall next to an ornate dark teak prayer bench. I'd never met the man who was talking rapidly to me on the phone. He mentioned the name of a woman I knew from Susannah's dinner parties. He was an orchid enthusiast. He'd heard from the man at Kew what I had and that it was flowering, then asked around until he found the personal connection. He sent a note round, then he called. He told me how much he would pay for one of my plants. I hesitated, astonished, and he raised the price, thinking he hadn't set it high enough.

He offered to come and get it. "No. I'll deliver it." I wanted to keep this from Cornelius. That worked in my favour too. The buyer thought I was being secretive about my growing methods and what orchids I had. "Quite right," he said and gave me his address. In the end, I made all the deliveries, usually by Underground or bus. I met some eccentric people and saw a great many orchids. Susannah, the freethinker, thought I was shopping and let me go anywhere. I went while Zoë was at Miss Bishop's.

The people who bought my plants wanted the orchids but did not always want to bother finding out what to do with them, so part of what I was selling was the knowledge I'd picked up from the few books I had read since the crate first arrived and what I learned from trial and error working with the plants. I used Susannah's typewriter, which was in a small office or large closet at the top of the stairs, to type out instructions on cards: add a little rough peat or spaghum moss mixed with charcoal; allow to get nearly dry; one plant may have 30 to 50 blossoms for seven weeks kept in a drawing room with fires only in the afternoon. This typewriter, the old Remington, became mine when Susannah died. And this is the typewriter on which I'm bashing this out on now.

"You know Mary Margaret is making money with those flowers?" said Mrs. Perry to Susannah one day in her grating voice, speaking as if I wasn't there in the room drinking tea with them.

"Oh it's just pin money."

"I suppose it's all right, her being a colonial?"

"It's a little hobby. A pleasant occupation. She looks so well."

"Oh yes. She looks well." They peered at me as though I were a vase, a thing, a bird in a cage.

Susannah tossed this off in public but appeared at the door of my room later. "Mary Margaret?" I threw a scarf over the coins and bills on the bed. I'd been counting them, running them through my fingers.

"What's this I hear about you making pots and pots of money? It doesn't seem quite right. You know you get your trust money when you marry or turn twenty-five?"

"I'm not going to marry."

"Of course you are." Susannah touched my hair, my shoulder, my hand, then turned away.

Zoë knew about the money. I had to tell someone. I asked if she could keep a tremendous secret and she nodded solemnly and gave a little salute. She watched wide-eyed as I tumbled the loot out on the bed.

"Where did you get that?"

"I've been saving them from my flowers."

"Oh, Mary-Margaret, what for?" little tiny voice, picking up one coin, one bill at a time and turning it over and over, reading it. We really didn't see much money, despite how spoiled we were.

"They're to send me to medical school."

"Away?"

"I'm afraid so darling."

"Then I hate them." But she didn't turn away from the coins, instead began lifting them and letting them fall onto the bed in a silver fountain as I had so many times.

"But you won't tell will you?"

"Nooo."

"Cornelius would be furious and Susannah upset."

"I know." Small voice.

Just before I retired, in fact the very week I retired from my long practice as a doctor, I saw an orchid at a florist's shop when I stopped to get something for my office nurse. It was a Phalaenopsis, not a fancy orchid at all. But something in the warmth and humidity of the shop and the sweet smell on the air, made my throat constrict and I thought for a time that I would grow orchids again when I retired. I could afford it. I understand that now they grow orchids under fluorescent lights, at least according to a Dr. Aphrodite J. Hofsommer who writes about it in the American Orchid Society Bulletin, which I don't get but saw at the library. For a time I looked at catalogues for glass houses. But I never had one built and I never went back.

Orchids with their sexual folds. Since I came to know the look of women's (and men's) bodies quite well in my practice, I saw it was true that orchids were sexual. The bulbs just like male orchids hanging. When we have to cut off a man's testicles we call it an orchidectomy. The orchids seemed to come from a time in my life when sex was still a possibility, the scent of sweetness, the humidity, all that was full of possibility. I don't think I could have stood it when I retired at seventy.

Just before I left that house and England, I sold all my orchids and a man came and carried them off in a van. Many of the orchids, like so many of the men, died in the War. My man died in the War and my orchids, though neither of them was mine anymore. You could say I lost nothing. The orchids had all been bought by Sir James Graham and moved to his estate in Devon. He was an acquaintance of Susannah's friend Mrs. Rees-Smith and I heard from Susannah that the orchids had died because they could not get enough coal to keep the stove going. I guess the interest had gone too, since three of the Graham sons were killed in the war. Hugo was killed at the Marne. Some orchids in Europe were bombed. During the Second War, the Botanical Museum at Dahlem in Berlin was bombed and at the end of the Japanese occupation of the Philippines, the Philippine National Herbarium was looted and burned.

When I stopped working with the orchids I stopped completely.

TEN

My father told me when I was a child that if I wanted to be a doctor when I grew up I could go to Bishop's Medical School in Lennoxville not far from Montreal. He was glad to say that they had started taking women medical students since stuffy old McGill wouldn't, and he and my brother had both gone to Bishop's. Now it seems extraordinary to me that he encouraged me and, despite my claims of persisting against universal disapproval, he at least must have humoured me. Perhaps I would have done nothing without that.

In 1901, after I started earning my own money, I wrote secretly to Bishop's applying to be a medical student. I watched the mail long before the reply could come, much as I had watched for Hugo's postcards. And it finally did come on a hot day in early August. Bishop's had stopped accepting women in 1900.

The Modern Age

Shortly after that letter came, I got up one morning with a pressure on my heart. My whole body felt bruised and aching. Hugo was gone. I was denied what I had always wanted. It seems I was to be nothing, an old maid, a crushed bug all my life. I went down through the garden to the greenhouse and spoke to my orchids. There were many in bloom and some just finishing. I did no work there that day but went from plant to plant, touching each elaborate bloom and bending close to inhale the lemony scent. Perhaps it is foolish but I am an old woman and don't care, so I will say it: I softly said goodbye to each bloom and stem. Goodbye Goodbye. I loved you in my way.

Then I went back and tried to eat breakfast. After that, I telephoned to the nursery man who had been pestering me about the orchids and set a price that was twice as high as we had ever spoken of. I said they must come and get them right away and bring the money with him.

That afternoon I purchased a ticket on the steamship 'Brautigan', leaving in two days for New York, and I began to pack. Why didn't I take Zoë with me? Could I have?

They came for the orchids the next morning with a big square truck. It was hot, August in London, hot for August even, so they came very early. It took two men with dirty fingers and overalls only an hour to pack them up carefully into the van. I watched stony-faced.

Where was Zoë that day? I cannot remember.

I am my own person. I am my own, I muttered through clenched teeth. How if I could have survived and stayed, I would have. But I couldn't survive there.

Zoë was abandoned, an abandoned child, a waif, well-dressed always and fed, and even educated, but a waif whom men wanted to protect and hurt. And then as she grew older, an abandoned woman.

I admired her. My life was so straitened. I didn't know before I started and only realized much later what the cost would be for me of being a "lady doctor". I was allowed to practise, to be a doctor, only under the strict condition that I be man-like, not unladylike, but stoic, never tearful, not emotional, not at all sexual, or sensual, or flirtatious, or pretty, or young, or unsure, or fragile. I must wear only the most severe of costumes, a skirt, heavy shoes, a jacket. No skin must show. My skirt lengths rose sedately with the times, my shoulders padded out and back. I could be jolly but not funny, smart but not too smart, sympathetic, but not vulnerable.

I can imagine another, better life, in which I took Zoë with me. We figured it all out, the impossibilities I couldn't imagine overcoming. Her wildness was tempered by my love and she married and had boys and stayed alive and grew old along with me. What a fool, even in imagination, to think that my love could have saved her when there seemed to be some kind of demon loose in the world. An alternative path that would have stopped the War from happening, the next war, the Holocaust, all that we came to know. If I had taken Zoë with me that day, onto the ship, there would have been peace along the borders, no military build-up, no assassination in Sarajevo, none of the insanity. Because Zoë, the New Woman would have been able to grow up in the New World.

I admired Zoë, I envied her womanly ways. I mean later when she grew up. Her beautiful strangely-coloured clothes, her insistence on drawing conclusions from her feelings. I admired her sureness, her freedom, her intensity. She was the New Woman. I admired the New Woman. I was the Old Woman pushing at some immovable gates. She didn't recognize the gates and simply leapt over convention. She was entirely unconventional. I was stuck.

Now I'm mildly eccentric and wear cotton pants and wool sweaters in all weathers. The kids think I'm dotty and perhaps I am.

Perhaps I wouldn't have gone, not had the courage.

The Modern Age

Perhaps I shouldn't have gone the way I did. If I had burned the recipe symbolically rather than in the real fire, perhaps I would have stayed. I was so angry about it all. I was for science and things being real, not humbug. I was for rational knowing. I felt I had to be in order to earn my place as a physician.

I left on the night of Coronation Day. It was August 9, 1902, the coronation of King Edward and Queen Alexandra, with its swirling sunlit display, its Fijians in petticoats and Red Indian chiefs in feathers and blankets, its Calvary, its crimson robes, its pale and finely drawn king, was he well enough? He was. Cornelius insisted that we go out and line up in the early morning on the parade route. We packed food in a large basket and took chairs and thermoses of tea and camped on the mall to take in the blur of colour and sound: Scotch pipes, Arabs in white flowing robes and turbans, carrying on their heads sections of guns, stopping suddenly and putting them together, a prolonged undertone of applause all along the mall as the King and new Queen in her purple velvet passed in the gilded glass coach., the national anthem taken up by one voice and then many, passed along the crowd. The Empire in flow.

Something about it -- the end of the Victorian age, the beginning of the Edwardian age, the demonstration that it was a big world, the excitement, I don't know what. I decided that day to go, to act. Even though I'd already bought my ticket out, that day I decided to do it. Deciding in stages. Decided at the Coronation.

That night I went to talk to Cornelius again.

Now I feel that in fairness I should try to think more clearly about Cornelius. Cornelius and Susannah. For so many years, the image of a Cornelius collapsed and sunk in ruin was not something I could afford to acknowledge. The bare fact of him is that he committed suicide in 1907 when his financial affairs collapsed in the depression of that year. How could he?

Who was Cornelius really? He was sociable, he loved

harmony. He loved the institutions of which he was always the head, the leading light: the Empire, the Church, the Family. He was a good warm host. He would call people by name after one introduction, attending to their needs, making sure they were comfortable. He was a story teller; most of his tales were family stories, told over and over, little things: the time Aunt Lavender mistook her umbrella for a snake, the day his mother got sick and died in one day. He had a kind of contagious pessimism. If he had a cold, the whole house was in gloom. And he was generous, and sometimes critical and carping at Susannah. I suppose he blamed himself for losing the family fortune. It turned out it wasn't as bad as he thought, but it was too late for him. He shot himself with a hunting gun. It was put out that it was an accident.

This is Cornelius: he smokes like Santa, jokes, has long legs, cruel eyes, silk ties, expects attention, dogs attend him drooling. He's always warm and furred, other men lift logs for him, women wash his clothes, he eats.

Now that I'm old and he long dead, it's time for compassion; how'd he get this way? Compassion comes hard from this crouching position.

Crouching because what he did that night has never left me. I often had to be out at night in the years I was delivering babies. And I never went out into the night without that sense of being braced against danger, no matter how benign this little town on the West Coast. It was the fear of being attacked which started I am sure that night that Cornelius hit me.

I should have known better. I now realize he was drunk. I didn't know then about the effects of alcohol. Cornelius must have been often drunk. What we took for his peculiarities in his fine clothes and buffered life must have been what on a poor man would have been judged the most degenerate drunkenness. It was Coronation Night. He was so proud of the British Empire and had been celebrating all day, drinking whisky and much wine at dinner, port with cigars.

The Modern Age

I went to his study after dinner, after their friends had left in a skirl, their war cry on the steps: money and more money. The Edwardian age would be good to them.

It was a mistake. Bad timing. But I was excited by the day too and I too had been drinking wine at dinner. Shame on me. Shame. I should have known better. I should have protected myself. I stood once again at his desk and told him I had enough money to send myself to medical school and I wanted his permission. Idiot. Again. And again he flourished that receipt that had made us so comfortable. I took it from his hand and looked this time. It was a recipe for cough syrup, called Doctor Howard's, which had been well marketed and had now made us rich, a scrawl in brown fading ink on thick paper with common ingredients, comfrey, horehound, sage, and peppermint in a base of alcohol. To me it seemed a hoax and that the whole thing was built on fraud. Quackery, and Cornelius taunting me, saying my idea of going to medical school was a waste of time because people were stupid and gullible. "Something came over me". I put that sentence in quotations because it is a cliché but it is true, that is what happened. Something swept through my body and caused it to flush and tremble. I turned, as though in slow motion and threw the recipe for wealth on the softly burning fire behind me.

Cornelius looked at me for a second with his eyes bugging out, slowly put down his cigar in the large ashtray, and came slowly up out of his chair and around the desk. I didn't know enough to run. I turned slightly to face him. He was bigger than me by head and shoulders. I've always been small and he was a big man. His big arm went slowly back then hit me hard. He cuffed me across the head with his open hand. His hand was big, the red mark and the bruise later went from the bottom of my chin all up my cheek and my ear rang and my head hurt. I fell against the green wing chair and crouched in it on my knees, silent. He took me by the arm and pulled me up hard and gave me a push towards the door. I caught a flash of his face. He was red and bursting with the effort not to kill me. He pushed and I fell. He kicked hard at my legs and buttocks

The Modern Age

with his leather-booted feet until I had crawled out the open door then he slammed it hard against the soles of my slippers. I looked up and there was Susannah in the doorway of her study, looking. She shook her head and turned away.

In my room I sat for some time on my bed, panting, touching my cheek. Then I got out the clothes I had taken from my brother when he died, the dark suit, the shirt, the socks, the shoes. I put on the pants, the socks, the dark leather shoes. I bound my breasts with the large lavender scarf I had bought with my first orchid money and put on the shirt. The fringe of the scarf bounced percussive against my belly as I turned. Then Susannah was in the room, still shaking her head, silent. My hair hung out of all its fastenings. Susannah took out the pins and turned around the room until she found my sewing scissors and cut it off, cut off my woman hair in long dark loops.

Silence is her weapon, her defense. She cuts my hair in silence, in silence lets me go. Now I wonder what she told him, how she sold him on my leaving. Twitch. The attention of the silent. Twitch. And later how she called his name, called his name when all her other words were swallowed whole. Dry hair and twitch. My chest hurts, Susannah. How I went through your things when you died looking for clues, for answers.

Then Zoë was there. She didn't say a word, just looked. She was twelve, a girl-woman, still a child, aware. She'd had lice in her dark hair because she went to school after all. She smelled of lice soap and her hair was wet. Her face that night hardened forever. Contagious how I never cried. She took my hair and stuffed it in a bag and threw it down the laundry chute, not one lock saved. And she was angry, holy anger. Just to have her for a moment for a moment to say holy holy anger, baby child. The feel of her hands on my hair, the absence of the feel of her hands on my hair is my penance baby child.

I went out into the night with the suitcase they packed for me, Susannah and Zoë, my money in a belt on my waist under my man jacket. I left as a man. I never saw Cornelius again.

Now I'm old, and all the tears I never shed are still in my body, a lump here on what's left of my breast. This lump shoots pain, a stab in my heart. And yet, through it all, something funny, a strange feeling blooms, a strange orchid in a foreign place. I'm not sure what it is. Perhaps this is what people call joy.

ELEVEN

And so I set out again across the ocean by steam ship, in the freedom of my brother's suit, my breasts flattened by a soft lavender scarf but my waist free and my edges hard. I cultivated a firm handshake and crossed my legs with my ankle on my knee. I took up smoking. (Smoking still, my small vice which I enjoy so much.) I tried to take up space, to interrupt conversations. That's what Cornelius did. But it was easier to be silent, to cultivate a wise demeanour and let people think what they wanted. I learned to walk with wide steps, to stand unevenly, weight on one leg with my hip cocked. I started out only with the idea of travelling safely as a small woman all alone.

On board ship, after I finished being sick, which took only one day, I enjoyed the costume. Being a man was a bit of an act anyway. Cornelius's act. My father's. A series of gestures, subtle or not so subtle. I didn't try to change my voice at all, since I couldn't force it below a certain range. But no one seemed to care. Whenever I was uncertain how to act as a man, I thought of Cornelius. I brought to mind his way of showing who he was, his sentences which fell hard at the ends with certainty, the pursing of his lips in judgment, the folding of his arms and rocking back on his heels.

I traveled first class in order to have a cabin to myself. The bald steward said nothing even though he must have wondered about the one masculine suit, the feminine underwear, and lack of luggage. He was totally discrete and silent, as was the tailor I later found in Montreal. It made me wonder whether they'd seen other strange beings like myself, and had said nothing, were utterly not astonished. Having money helped, I know that. Later, as a doctor, I saw a few strange beings myself.

I was on holiday all at once. Everything had happened so quickly. I was suddenly free of the necessity to worry about greenhouse pests: red spider, thrips, mealy bugs, white scale, brown scale, cockroaches. But I missed the orchids. I had thirteen of Zoë's beautiful water colour drawings of the flowers: on one a spike with nine perfect flowers, each with detailed lines and shades, and on another plant, thirty flowers. I sat for long minutes, or perhaps hours, in the shimmer of the mid-Atlantic sun, looking at these small paintings, wondering at the calm that had descended on my life. I was going forward alone and was apparently not afraid. At first I did not think much about those left behind. I was calm, in a trance. After dinner, I stood out on the deck, smoking, and was amazed to be there under the stars, in the cold air, alone.

I was seated at dinner with a man who introduced himself as Percival Campbell. He was flamboyant in his dress

The Modern Age

and speech, and apparently unrepentantly homosexual, travelling with his "secretary" Miles Wood, an artist and an actor, who did not speak much. Percival tapped the silver on the cloth and told long interesting stories of his travels collecting antiques for his villa in Sicily. He'd recently been to Korea to bring home six antique chests on the Trans-Siberian railway. Before that he'd been in China and Japan. I don't know where he got his money. He was beautifully dressed. His family was from Montreal but he lived with Miles Woods in the villa in Sicily.

I meant not to speak to my dinner companions about myself and my hopes. But Percival kept calling me "old chap" and was so warm and friendly that one night over brandy, I blurted out that I was hoping to get into medical school at Bishop's. He threw up his hands with a noise I could only call a squeal and said, "Oh my cousin Archie is the head man there. He hasn't cut me off. I'll write you a letter and you'll have no problem."

I stayed in touch with Percy for many years, writing to him in Sicily, signing my name Martin, and receiving the odd amusing letter back, until I heard from Miles Wood a few years ago that he had died quietly and well, leaving the villa in trust to Miles and ultimately to the village. Now, so much later, I wonder whether Percy, with his well-developed homosexual sensitivity, did not guess the truth about me.

But when I landed in Montreal, I was uncertain what to do. I'd heard that there were one or two universities, like Dalhousie in Halifax, that were now taking women medical students. Should I try one of them? Or stick to my original dream of going to Bishop's, as my father and brother had before me? Later I found out what it was like for women at that time at medical school, the taunting, the eggs thrown, the jokes, and I think I made the right decision. Maybe it was perverse or neurotic, as the Freudians would say, but I determined in the quiet first days alone in Montreal to try to go to my father's college. A Freudian field day no doubt.

Before I go on about medical school and all that, I feel I need to say a few things more on the subject of women dressing as men. I say I don't care what people think of me anymore but I feel a need to do a bit of explaining. It seems such an odd thing to have done.

The Bible is quite clear on the subject: in Deuteronomy 22:5 it says "woman shall not wear that which pertaineth unto a man, neither shall a man put on a woman's garment: for all that do so are an abomination unto the Lord thy God." But throughout the ages, and for various reasons, women have needed to pretend to be men. And though I knew I risked being an abomination unto the Lord at the time, I was willing to risk it, having already passed into and out of my Christian phase. I didn't and don't care what it says in the Bible.

"You have to keep them in their place." This was one of the commonplaces of the time and station. When I heard it uttered over his white whiskers by an elderly man at dinner on the ship crossing to New York, I realized I'd heard it many times before. "Oh yes, my dear," said Percy rolling his eyes, and tapping the thick white cloth with his salad fork, "keep them in their place." The elderly man's wife, sitting next to him, pursed her lips and nodded, not noticing Percy's sarcasm. The elderly man and his wife, the Kennedy-Smiths, appeared at table only once, apparently overcome after that with seasickness. We joked about them mercilessly. "Them" of course, who must be kept in their place, were the distaff side, the women, ladies. I don't know where I got the idea that I would be damned if I'd stay in my place, but somewhere along the way I did. Percy was wonderful putting on his Kennedy-Smith act. "I can out Kennedy-Smith the Kennedy-Smiths," he said.

All I knew about being a man, or a woman dressed as a man, was to spread my legs. I'd read Tom Sawyer (or was it Huckleberry Finn, I can't remember after all these years), where Tom (or Huck was it?) is discovered as not a real girl because he closed his legs to catch the sewing kit instead of spreading his skirt.

Later I learned that the tossed sewing kit was just one of many "tests" to determine whether there is a gender trick in the works. Tests to unmask a woman dressed as a man or a man dressed as a woman:

Place a spinning wheel nearby, woman is interested, man is not.

Throw a ball, woman spreads her legs to catch it, man does not.

Scatter peas on the ground, the man has a firm step the woman does not.

Most of the time in my masquerade, I felt that I was slipping on peas, not going to be able to stop myself if I started to fall. But it was fun, exhilarating somehow, fraudulent and fun for that. It made me feel more alive because of the risk of being caught, like a man in a fast car who may be risking his life. Of course eventually I was caught, but more of that later.

There are at least two reasons for a woman to dress as a man. I'll leave aside the complicated questions of women who feel more manly than womanly. Radclyffe Hall does that quite eloquently in her way. Aside from that, a woman may want to dress as a man for comfort, or for freedom, two related, but not identical tricks.

First on the subject of comfort. In 1880, the year I was born, a woman's dress covered her tightly from neck to knee. It was impossible to take large steps. Then came the bustle and huge wooden frames to bell out the skirts. I don't know how women sat or went through doorways. The hobble skirt. Whalebone stays. Now we have high heels and girdles of course. What I discovered is that the man's suit is a lovely garment to wear. It covers everything loosely. It's perfect for large movements; everything overlaps; there are no gaps. When you stop moving, everything just falls back into place.

The Modern Age

Great for a dash for the streetcar, or a brief struggle with a crazed patient.

Over the years of the Nineteenth and early Twentieth Centuries, various ladies worked towards dress reform based on comfort and hygiene. Whether by their efforts or by some kind of divine evolution, by the time I was a lady, our clothing had become more reasonable. The tailored suits and loose skirt and blouse combinations were a huge improvement on the bustles of the generation before mine. And the bicycle had made a big difference in freeing up women's clothes. Some women, quite outrageously, even wore pants.

I was back in Europe, in Paris for a holiday, in the lovely false summer of 1914. This was one of the few times I was glad to dress as a lady and felt the whole fashion thing to be worth it. In Paris that summer I put aside my practical doctor clothes after ten years of practice and dressed in what the other ladies were wearing: black satin silk and chiffon made into thin frocks. Black and white were the colours; we wore wide hats and carried frilly sunshades. The men wore dark gray morning coats with light striped gray trousers, and abundant ties with scarf pins. They carried glossy tall hats, which they left under chairs. I sat with a woman doctor from Paris in the fashionable restaurant Armenonville in the Bois de Bologne, under a canvas tent over a wooden floor while a tail-coated orchestra played syncopated tunes. This is a bittersweet memory. I was thirty-four. It was perhaps the last time I felt it was possible to be a woman who might attract a man. And I did. Soon after that, war was declared and Zoë was dead.

During the War, things changed so much for women. After the War, skirts shortened dramatically, hair was cut and legs exposed. Some thought the whole thing quite ugly. I don't know myself. But everything was changed.

Now, as I think I've said, I wear only trousers. Wearing skirts as I did for all my years as a respectable woman doctor, letting them rise and fall with the fashion, made me feel helpless and hopeless. Wearing trousers makes me feel free. I'm sure most women have been quite happy to wear whatever fashion or the times has dictated; they've lived free happy fulfilled lives. Your psychoanalyst might take a look at my life and comment on the fact that I never married, that I never had children and think me less a woman, but I bled, I bruised like a woman. I had womanly fears and hopes. I just wanted to do something a bit different and I wanted to be free. When I first put on the soft wool outfit that they called a man's suit, I felt good and right and ready to move.

And that is the second reason why a woman might dress as a man and why they have done so throughout history, religion and convention be damned: there have been so many activities and motions and callings prohibited to women throughout the centuries. Sometimes we are in desperate economic circumstances, or something in our soul just calls us to something, to be a doctor, a lawyer, a soldier, a thief or a Pope. Why not?

There was Pope Joan, elected in the ninth century, a woman who dressed in monk's clothing, was so learned she was elected Pope, then died in childbirth during a solemn parade. Or so the story goes. And then the echo of her life: the 17th Century literary fascination and the novel Papissa Joanna in 1886. Maybe none of it was true, but so interesting.

Then this: the executioner of Lyon in 1749 betrayed herself while in a drunken state to be a woman. The moral: you can't afford to get drunk (or pregnant) when you have something to hide.

Susannah first told me about women soldiers. Now they are saying that there were 400 women fighting as men in the Union army in the American Civil War. One of them, Sarah Emma Seelye, alias Franklin Thomson, later became the first woman member of the Grand Army of the Republic, which became the American Legion.

The Modern Age

There've been at least two books about Mountain Charley, a legendary woman trapper disguised as a man trapper in the Wild West of the United States.

Hundreds of Russian women were disguised as men during World War One.

Some women dressed as men have even courted and married other women. Some made up fake penises and peed through a horn.

Well I've gotten pedantic, but I made a bit of a study of all this, probably to justify my strange behavior. My trailbreaker through all this, my model, was the first woman doctor in Canada, Dr. James Barry, or Miranda Stuart, who was the medical officer in Upper Canada in 1857 and led a swashbuckling life all over the world as a man and was only discovered to be a woman when she died. They say she was only five feet tall with a big nose and a strutting walk. When she died, the woman who laid her out, a Mrs. Bishop, declared there were clear signs she'd had a child. Mrs. Bishop knew the signs for she'd had nine herself.

Anyway, about the fourth day out from England, in the middle of the summer Atlantic, I decided to try to do it this way, to go on dressing the part. At that point, I was having fun with it. I was a small man in a heavy coat. My rich clothing was authoritative, if sometimes a bit out of fashion. I always wore a very clean white shirt. My landlady in Montreal did my shirts for me. I found a discrete tailor.

I used Percival's letter of introduction and was invited to meet the Dean of Bishop's Medical School, Doctor Archibald Campbell, in his large book-lined study in downtown Montreal. It was a good thing I didn't really understand what power this man would have over my life as a medical student, or I would have been trembling too much. He read the letter and said tolerantly, "Ah yes, Percy. He's a fruit you know." He asked if I was related to Dr. George Howard (my father). I said he was my uncle and that I'd come from

England to train where he'd trained, and make my way in the New World. That pleased Doctor Campbell and he talked for some time about my father and grandfather and how he'd known them since he came to Montreal in the 1880's and how they were fine people. I remembered then my father speaking often and approvingly about Dean Campbell. It wasn't until the middle of the interview that I realized it was this Dean Campbell, this man. Percival's "Uncle Archie" was my father's "Dean Campbell".

On the basis of all this mutual regard, he waved off my lack of formal education. (I said I'd been educated privately) and said I'd do fine and accepted me into the program on the spot.

The first misconception I had to deal with was that I would be going to school in Lennoxville in the Eastern Townships where my brother had gone. He'd told me wonderful tales of the low open bridge across the Massawipi River at what had earlier been a fording place. He told me about the skating rink, the cricket, boating on the Massawipi and the time he had narrowly missed being capsized by a large cake of ice. The idea of studying, as my brother had, in a cold room by lamplight while the water froze in the bowl took on extraordinary glamour. But it turned out the medical school itself was in Montreal in the middle of the city. I'd never talked to my father about where he actually studied. I realized I'd have to get rooms. I wonder now, did I actually think I would have pulled off this dressed as a man thing for even twenty-four hours living in residence with a pack of young men?

However, after I adjusted to the fact that I'd be staying in Montreal, it went smoothly, like a dream. I found a flat up three flights of stairs where the landlady provided meals -- watery gravy and mushy peas. Brick and ivy. Even now when I see a house like that red brick with ivy and the dirty curtains at the windows I get a nauseated feeling, the feeling of loneliness and greasy food.

I was lonely. I lived for Zoë's letters which came in

bunches once every three weeks or so. She wrote funny stories about the dogs and about what she was learning in school and nothing at all about Cornelius or Susannah.

But it was good. I tasted freedom, learned about money for the first time, that is learned to be careful about money. For the first time in my life it occurred to me that money was hard to earn and easy to spend. I had two suits and four shirts. Every dollar was thought over carefully.

I studied on my own for a few weeks, wrote a grueling series of Matriculation exams, and was accepted into Bishop's Medical Faculty as Martin M. Howard. I walked through the elegant portico at Bishop's Medical School at Ontario and St. George Street on October 2, 1902.

As Mr. Howard, I studied Anatomy, Chemistry, Materia Medica, and Therapeutics. Undetected, I learned about Midwifery and the Diseases of Women and Children. I did Surgery, Medical Jurisprudence, and Pathology. The medical men knew there was something queer about me and left me alone. For some reason I loved the dissecting room, a 30-foot long room on a corner with light coming in from two sides. I didn't faint the first time our professor cut into a cadaver, as some of the men did. I was cold-blooded about that kind of thing. Knife into flesh. I might have been a surgeon if I was a man. I did love putting my hands on the pregnant women though. I sat by myself with my books in the second story reading room, smoking and studying. I learned to hold my pee for long periods until I could be alone in a bathroom.

My remembrance of those first weeks is of walking in the almost dark streets in the cold rain of early winter, head full of anatomy and pictures of bodies in their wrinkled varied forms. It was afternoon, after class, but the sky almost dark. Collar pulled up, wind blowing cold rain and sleet into my face. My feet were wet and I was near tears, just gritting my teeth. The rain went on and on and then it snowed and was very cold. I walked into the medical school smoking room one day near the beginning and Jones was standing with his pants down to his knees, showing the other men his equipment, bare behind, pimpled and hairy towards the door.

"Silly ass," I said and backed right out.

What do men talk about when they are alone, away from women? Sports, girls, killing people, beer and getting drunk, medical stuff, cadaver jokes, ejaculating, politics, fishing, hunting, bird-watching, how attractive their lady friends are, cars. Men are heavy mannish thick-moustached and sleepy. Or childish, roughhousing with each other like little boys. How different they are when they are with a woman or one of the more civilized professors. I grew to like them in a funny way.

After six months, I made a friend, someone almost as strange as I was, another outsider. He was Hébert, a French-Canadian from Saint Jovite, just north of Montreal. He was the only French Canadian in the medical school as far as I could tell. And he stood out because of his size, about six and a half feet tall and big all over. This was how we made friends: he stabbed me in the hand. It was during a dissecting exercise and we had been paired up, as we had been before, the two outsiders. He was preoccupied, not looking what he was doing. I was holding open the chest of the man's body we were working on and he cut without looking and slashed into the fleshy part below my thumb. It bled profusely. He was aghast and pulled out his handkerchief to wrap it, but it still bled.

"I'll go and call a doctor," he said.

"No don't call a doctor." I certainly didn't want anyone listening to my heart, or telling me to take my shirt off. "Just put some rubbing alcohol on it."

"I don't have any rubbing alcohol." He looked around the room in a panic. "Wait," he said and ran out. I just sat there, holding my hand, too shocked to move. One minute later, he was back with a small silver flask in his huge hand. He poured a generous splash into the wound, which had now almost stopped bleeding, and offered me the flask. I took a small swig - it was white rum - and passed it back. He drank heavily, then sat down hard on the stool beside me and we both started laughing.

The next day, after the Anatomy lecture, he approached me and began speaking in his heavily accented English, apologizing again and explaining that he had been preoccupied with family worries and he was deeply sorry. Perhaps a man wouldn't have asked and if I had been really careful I shouldn't have, but I asked what the trouble was and he told me about his mother being ill and his sister pregnant. After that he often walked with me between classes or to the place where our paths home diverged. He did not try to become more intimate than that, nor did I. He was an outsider and I was and yet we became good friends.

We sat together, two out of 150 students in the lecture room. We walked to the library and sat across the table from each other. We smoked together in the student's waiting room. We walked together over to Women's Hospital on Antoine St. for the Midwifery demonstrations. We became friends. We were both strange, we laughed. His large quiet presence protected me from the other men. How do I know that? Because after he became my friend, the hostility towards me lessened. How do I know that? I don't know. I just felt it. When you walk at night with a large dog, even the most friendly dog in the world, people are more careful.

But the men were like children, full of pranks and tricks and loud voices. Every once in a while one of them, tipping his wooden chair, would crash. The other men clapped and laughed their loud male laughs. Hébert and I would roll our eyes. They called us The Twins, though we looked nothing alike. That was their joke. How can I complain about the men's laughs being too loud and unrestrained when I felt it awful that women should be compelled to restrain their laughs? I don't make sense.

I didn't feel it was safe to drink because I would get

loosened and caught but I went out with the men sometimes, and sat quietly smoking while they got drunk and talkative and rowdy. Later Hébert and I helped many of them to bed after a night of silly songs and throwing up on the street.

As I said, I grew to rather like men after my years among them. Before I got to see them up close this way, men were like Cornelius, overbearing, mean, and jolly; or like Hugo, tender and crazy. I couldn't live with either of them apparently. At medical school I saw men were just silly little boys. Their doggy smells. These men, away from women used ugly words, as though it was wonderful to be naughty. They loved blasphemy. They were shameless talkers. They spoke lovingly of pipe smoking and fishing and not at all about their fears or sorrows. Their humour was macabre and really sharp. Later, at medical conventions, which I attended as often as I could, for I loved to travel, I saw that the boys who became men didn't actually grow up; they just grew wider and greyer. I hate speaking this way, it is so harsh, and mostly untrue for there are many fine men. Now Morgan, still childish in so many ways, has this sweetness that I cherish so much. Stupid to try to write about men as one thing.

TWELVE

I was found out in my disguise twice, possibly three times. Then the men, my fellow students suffered me on the borderline between man and woman, deeply puzzled. But before I tell how that happened, I feel I must make another longish, somewhat pedantic, digression.

Now, writing in 1965, it seems outrageous that it was so difficult for a woman, even one with money of her own, to do the simplest thing, that is train to be a doctor. It is still not accepted at all that women can make good doctors, can go about delivering babies and administering antibiotics without doing violence to their tender selves, but then it was outrageously difficult. I feel I must give some context to this, to give a little history of women at medical school.

On January 23, 1849, at Geneva Medical College in Geneva, New York, Elizabeth Blackwell earned the first MD by a woman anywhere in the world. Geneva College then immediately closed its doors to women. She graduated at the top of her class but was declared a freak whose unnatural example ought not to be followed by other women. During her training, doctor's wives refused to speak to her and the people of Geneva, New York stared. She was subjected to ribald jokes in connection with the dissections of the male reproductive system. She was accused of being lewd, insane, and a bad influence on children. She was promised letters of recommendation, which were never sent. In his valedictory speech the head of the school called the students "Gentlemen" as if there were no ladies there.

Later he wrote: "Generally ladies do not have the moral, physical, and intellectual qualifications necessary for discharging the duties of our calling. Instances occasionally happen where a female displays these qualities. It would be unwise and unjust to withhold from them those advantages and honours due the rest. However I feel bound to say that the inconveniences attending the admission of females to all lectures in medical school are so great that I shall on all future occasions oppose such a practice." And he did.

Men said that the exception, Elizabeth Blackwell, proves the rule, and asked, "Are there no masculine females?" That is, Male minds in Female bodies? She did very well, but most would not.

There were two main strands to the argument against training women to be doctors. One was that they weren't strong enough. Edward Clark wrote in 1869 that women have the right, but not the ability, to practice medicine, particularly at a certain time of the month. This argument was usually elaborated at length with much show of concern for the well being of the tender sex. Personally, the first time I watched a woman give birth I realized that the talk of the tender sex and the fragility of women was a sham and wondered why such talk existed. Possibly to protect the tenderness of men. I wondered if women were to be kept from becoming doctors because it would be too frightening for the men to know that women knew the truth about who was strong and who was not.

The other argument against women becoming doctors was that it would be immoral for women to listen to talk about male genitalia, to dissect male bodies, to discuss anatomy with men, to perform any medical or surgical procedure. This argument was stated delicately, not elaborated, and referred to with much pursing of lips and downcast eyes.

Nevertheless, women were starting to be accepted at some medical schools, mostly in Europe. Zurich first permitted women to study medicine in 1864. Bern and Geneva in 1872.

In Canada, as schools opened their doors to women (and often enough shut them again), the women suffered offence after offence: feces on the seats they usually sat in, obnoxious sketches on the wall, objectionable stories by lecturers, and noisy vulgar demonstrations. Some women were pushed down into the mud. All were subjected to lewd remarks and crude behavior from their fellow students.

Nevertheless, some women persisted.

In 1876, Charlotte Whitehead Ross opened a practice for women and children in Montreal. She took ten years to graduate as her studies were broken by family tragedies, pregnancies, and miscarriages. She was pregnant when sitting her finals and had her fifth child three months after graduation. She did her thesis on abortion. Afterwards she joined her husband in a railway camp in Manitoba where she mostly treated logging accidents and ax wounds. She loved nice clothes and ordered things from Montreal. Unlike most of us "lady doctors", she was a "womanly woman" who had eight children. She gave birth to her last child when she was almost fifty.

Victoria Ernst graduated from Dalhousie in 1900 when she was forty-four. She adopted the most difficult boys in the orphanage but never married. She took up real estate and became wealthy.

In 1882 fifty male medical students from Queen's College in Kingston threatened to leave Queen's unless female students were excluded from their classes. The women were excluded.

In 1890 women were accepted at Bishop's, and facilities were prepared for them at a cost of $720. (McGill said it would cost $250,000). Basically they built a separate dissecting room. The seven women who attended were labelled "sweet girl medicos". Grace Ritchie was the first lady graduate in 1891. She was then hired as the Demonstrator of Anatomy for Lady Students. At the Convocation in 1894, Maude Abbot took the prize for best final examination and was cheered and presented with bouquets of flowers. In 1897, the faculty voted to refuse to admit any more lady students. One final lady student was admitted in September 1898 on the understanding she would not be permitted to attend for more than the two years. In 1900, the last lady doctor graduated from Bishop's Medical School. "Women were more trouble than they were worth," the administration said.

That first year of training I went to a talk by Dr. Emily Stowe, the first Canadian woman to practise in Canada. She was plump and outspoken, with an aggressive lower lip, fanatical eyes, and round glasses. She was trained in the U.S., and had to practice illegally in Toronto for the first three years. In 1870 the Toronto School of Medicine admitted her and Jennie Trout so she could get her Canadian credentials. They had to agree to make no fuss, no matter what happened. The walls had to be whitewashed four times during that session because of lewd sketches. Emily Stowe was still unable to get a license until 1880. Her daughter, Augusta Stowe, was the first woman to earn a Canadian degree. This training was so awful for her that she often cried herself to sleep.

Medical school. The lecture theatre with its flimsy wooden chairs and mildew smell. The lecturers, men in dusty coats with hair on their faces and absolute sureness in their delivery. God-like men. Compared to them, Cornelius was soft and tentative, hesitating with his puffy lips. Of course they weren't all alike. Doctor Wilson was big like a large animal with meaty hands, which he ran through his hair. I always thought his hands must feel greasy afterwards. When he did that I looked away. It was more disgusting to me than the most putrid corpse. I looked up at the dirty windows, high up.

One day, Dr. Wilson's wife came and sat outside while he lectured. It was a clear autumn day that brought on wind, leaves lifting and turning, rain in fits, a sense of cold coming on. Poplar leaves rattled in the wind. That day he gave us a tirade about women who wanted to be doctors, quoting St. Paul, full of sarcasm and derision, putting on a show for his wife. The Almighty never intended for women to become physicians, he said in conclusion. Did he look at me? I don't know.

Anatomy, physiology, obstetrics, dissection, pharmacy, men and boys, autumn, winter, spring, summer, autumn, winter, spring.

And so I graduated as a Medical Doctor two years later. Now it takes four years. The convocation was in the Synod Hall behind Christ Church Cathedral and I proudly wore the scarlet and blue silk hood. I never got a gold-handled cane, the traditional emblem of the medical and surgical professions. It would have been ridiculous. But I decided after that to make my way as a woman. I got my degree as M. Howard and I got on a train headed west.

The Modern Age

My hair is grey and stringy now, thin and almost gone. I practised for forty-eight years here in Vancouver. Practised through the flu epidemic in 1918 and 1919, not getting sick, staying well. Thirty thousand people in Vancouver caught the flu; 900 died. I stayed well by the skin of my neck, skin of my teeth. Called out at night for babies in my dark car with doctor plates. Come back to the car and find the window smashed, the bag gone, the seats slashed. Why? So much anger loose in the world.

Now my legs are stiff, my fingers bent with arthritis. Every day something more is taken from me. But I hardly notice. Sleep is hard to come by. I carry money in my bra. Thank heaven for how underwear has changed over the years. I wear sweaters and pants and shirts and thick-soled shoes and socks and gloves. My hip is sore and the side of my face is sore.

I look around. How did I get here? I'm surrounded by furniture from my parents' house in Montreal.

I still have my black doctor's bag, equipped and ready, though I never take it from the cupboard now. The leather bag is flat-bottomed, curved up to the top with stiff leather-covered handles. It opens wide at the top. In it are: stethoscope, thermometer, hammer, aspirin, sulfa drugs, rubbing alcohol, pen, prescription pads, bandages. It is lined with maroon silk, stained and quite worn. The leather is deeply wrinkled with dust in the wrinkles. I'm proud of these stains and wrinkles of use. They represent years of careful doctoring. My housekeeper tries to keep the old leather bag clean. It has square hard handles and a brass clasp with a key, but I never locked it. Also: rubber gloves, washing solution, forceps.

I haven't written about how I was discovered as a woman but I am tired now so it will have to wait for another day. Here's hoping I have the strength to continue.

THIRTEEN

Damn. I fell on Saskia's patio. Coming down slate steps in sun, dazzled with reflections off the water, I thought I was on the bottom but there was one more step. Fell hard, face down on the slate, bruised my face, left arm, and right leg. Abrasions on my knees. I was shook. And I felt a complete ass. I still feel like a car wreck. That was three days ago. And my face is green and yellow all along one side. Lucky I didn't break my hip. That could have been it for me.

Damn damn damn. Also Morgan was there. I can almost cover the bruises with makeup, which I have from some long ago notion of dressing up. Yes I remember I got it for the banquet honouring me put on by the Medical Association.

They named a bursary in my honour and I thought the least I could do was make an effort, so I went out and bought some expensive makeup and Sarah tried to help me rig myself out in it. Anyway there's no good pretending with the makeup for Morgan. He was there and saw me go down. I almost treated *him* for shock. Saskia offered scotch and I think she'd been planning to give us beer. Now Morgan has more ammunition for his nursing home battle. At least he held off that day, bless him. But I'm expecting the full barrage next time I see him. He's phoned twice.

I'd almost forgotten Saskia. Well not forgotten. I'd never forget her, but our lives became quite different, we went different ways, so that even though we ended up in the same town we had to work to see each other. She ended up rich, married a man who became a lumber baron, became the kind of person you saw in the society pages, such as they were, organizing charity balls, and living on the waterfront in West Vancouver. And I was always working. The funny thing is that I was thinking about Saskia when she called to ask us to lunch, because she was the one who kept me sane through med school. Saskia and Hébert.

The first time I was revealed in my man disguise, it was by Saskia's little sister, I'll be darned if I can remember her name. Children are less easily fooled by cross-dressing, less conditioned to see the clothing as the person. Exposure felt dangerous then, but now I don't think it was. It came about because of my loneliness and my need for a woman friend.

If I was a better person, stronger, braver, more convinced of my need to forge my way, I would have been more like Miss King, as I knew her first. The college wouldn't register her, even though she was qualified. She came to classes anyway, convinced that one day soon they'd be bound to accept her and recognize her learning. She meant to wear them down by her persistence, a strong-minded female swinging a blue cotton umbrella. She worked in an office near the college and with her shoulders squared attended medical classes and demonstrations when she could, and when the doctors let her. She endured the most dreadful assaults and insults, some of them actually physical. These pleasant, fresh-faced young men apparently felt so threatened by a young strong-hearted woman among them that they bustled her, pushed her down, and threw mud on her clothing.

Miss King became my dear friend Saskia.

One day I watched one of these ugly exchanges from the sidelines. One of the students jostled her. She called out, "Ignorant lout!" as he ran away. I had to smile. I said, "You're a sharp-tongued individual."

"How else should I be in this place?" she threw back, brushing off her skirt.

That was the beginning of a somewhat barbed flirtation we carried on for about three months, with bows and exaggerated expressions of respect. "Miss King," I would say as I bowed.

"Mr. Howard," and she bowed back. I watched for her. She could only come occasionally, about one day a week. She grew to trust me a bit as a man because I never joined in the taunts. I blushed and bowed my head. I know she saw me. But I never defended her either. Later she told me that she knew she'd have to fight this battle alone and she had steeled herself to it. She didn't blame me, which was a blessing I felt I never deserved but was glad for anyway.

After a few weeks of these bows, and respectful greetings, I asked if I might walk with her from one class to another. She agreed. From then on, we often walked together, often the incongruous three of us, tall red-haired Scottish Saskia King, big dark-haired Hébert Paquette, and me. Finally one day she asked us to tea at her house. She lived with her mother and several younger siblings in a plain house in an unremarkable English neighbourhood. Her father had been a Scottish merchant and had died several years earlier, leaving them fairly comfortable.

What struck me immediately was how she softened as she walked through the door, how her mother's warmth and

The Modern Age

shelter allowed her hair to curl more softly, her shoulders to drop, her shape to become more womanly.

I guess the atmosphere had its effect on me too because I became a frequent visitor with and without Hébert. It was there that I finally allowed myself to be known as a woman though there were no tests put like the sewing kit thrown into Huck Finn's lap. It was a place where being a woman seemed to make sense. Mrs. King called me "dearie" and "sweetie" from the start and touched me without restraint. She was the fattest person I'd ever met and she baked all the time. She said she was baking for God and she didn't like a day to go by in which she did not do something for God and she had such a poor imagination that she mostly just baked. She made sugar cookies iced with bright coloured hard icing and butter tarts so sweet they hurt and many loaves of soft white bread.

One day I was sitting by the fire drinking tea and almost dozing. One of the little girls passed behind my chair and in passing ran her hands along my neck. She came back into the room a few minutes later and said, "Why do you dress so funny?" Mrs. King laughed and I caught Saskia's smile and realized that they knew. That frightened me. What if the men at the college knew? I didn't say anything. Saskia just grinned and shook her head as though to say don't worry. No one answered the little girl. I forget which one she was and sometimes at night try to remember those little girls' names. They were all different and I can remember them all quite well, but not what they were called.

That evening I realized that the hardness that Saskia shed when she came in the door was what I put on always in the world and it protected me quite well. It always made me wonder afterwards, since I spent so much of my time with men, working with them, and with men even as my patients, whether they went out of their houses armed this way and, if left to be natural, would be softer and sweeter. Since I've had no intimate relations with men since Hugo so long ago, and it is not something I've been able to ask anyone about, this has become one of those idle and rather silly thoughts that float around from time to time. Their house smelled of sausages and pastry cooking. A bakery in the Kerrisdale village has that smell.

•

The second time I was exposed was much more dangerous. It began with harmony: the men singing together. It was a good moment, a quiet time in the smoking room at the university. We were waiting until it was time to go to the maternity hospital for another lesson. One of the men started singing Fréré Jacques and the others joined in, for once not in a bawdy or sarcastic way, but sweetly. I looked up at Hébert, tall and dark, pale, and well-muscled, singing unselfconsciously with his whole body. At that moment I loved him, and I always loved him as my brother. For Hébert, everything was effortless. Later he got stout but then was just big. He had a loud laugh and big feet, and lines around his eyes already from smiling. Where do you get your shoes? I wanted to ask. He loved riding horses. He went fishing on the ice. He picked apples in an abandoned orchard and took them home to his mother. He was a sensualist.

Last night I had a dream. In the dream, a man is teaching me to sing. He is very close, but not really sexual. He listens, says, "It's better but still so effortful." "How can I make it less effortful," I say. "Keep trying," he says. Now I think that's quite funny. I sit here at my typewriter with my face bruised from falling and my funny little dog quiet on the floor beside me, and I laugh. Everything takes so much effort. In the rain and the dark. Keep trying. Keep trying to make it less effortful. The atmosphere is so dense here on earth.

But back then, just as the men were singing, I started to feel sick. It was a recurrence of my illness, the one I thought of as broken-heart, but which was otherwise mysterious. At first I felt nauseous and then hot. I realized I was sweating. Things were going out of control very quickly. The men got up to go to class and I got up to go with them but my legs wouldn't carry me. I forced myself. Hébert noticed. "Some ting wrong?"

But I couldn't answer. His voice came from very far away and then I was unconscious.

What happened after that I can only guess because no one ever told me or spoke of it. I guess that Hébert got me back to my rooms since that's where I was when I came to again. I suppose he sent the landlady's son to get Doctor Campbell (my Dean) and that he attended me there. I guess that I was in a fever and had sweated through my shirt and they took it off to wash me down and found me out. I know that Hébert was there when I came to and Doctor Campbell came in shortly after that. I assume they both knew. Hébert told me my fever had gone up to 104. I don't know about the landlady, whether she knew, but she also nursed me during this time. I was sick for almost ten days.

So I was discovered and I waited to be expelled from medical school. Dean Campbell came every day until I was well enough to get up, but he said nothing. After that first day of fever and unconsciousness, I kept myself wrapped and covered with the scarf, a shirt, and a dressing gown, no matter how weak I felt. I spent a long week of acute embarrassment and trepidation, then I realized Dean Campbell wasn't going to say anything, that if I kept up the appearance of being a man, he would keep up the appearance of believing me.

Why I wonder did this powerful head of medicine let it go, let me continue with my disguise? He said Percy's a fruit, and admitted me to the school. Did he know right from the start? Or did he think he had made a mistake and if he tried to correct it he would look like an idiot? I have no answers to these questions. I was grateful to continue unmolested.

What surprised me was what happened with Hébert. And it happened so fast and ended so fast, like a dream you can't quite remember. Did I imagine it? I think not.

The first day I was up and dressed, I felt much better but still quite weak. Hébert came in, filling up the room, an effect I hadn't noticed when I was flattened on the bed. I

The Modern Age

backed up a bit to let him in and closed the door. Suddenly he was pulling me towards him. He pressed me into his body with one large hand on my back, one on my flattened breast. His mouth came down towards mine. He had one of my arms pinned but my left was free. I pulled back and punched him as hard as I could in the stomach.

I don't suppose I made a dint but he let me go right away and backed off. And we stood staring at each other in shock across the small space of the room, both of us breathing hard. His eyes were wide shocked wheels of different colours: blue, green, brown, yellow. He said, "I want to marry you. You will be my wife. You can practice medicine in the Laurentian Mountains with me."

"No," I said, "Non, mon ami." I took his hand and led him to a chair. He sat heavily and sobbed once. For a moment I let the fantasy play out: live with Hébert in the Laurentians, walking on the frozen lake to work with the ice groaning beneath me, skiing, eating apples from his trees, knowing his family, being safe, maple syrup. "You're my friend," I said. I don't know how I knew that I could not be his wife but I did. Something about how it was with Hugo. Something had ruined me for Hébert.

And it's too bad. He was a good man. I'm grateful to him for how he was afterwards. If anything, our friendship deepened. And he never betrayed me, even though he was deeply hurt.

I needed a friend because Saskia King had moved away. She married her boss's son and moved to Toronto. It seemed all of a sudden. She gave up going to medical school, even though she could have gone to Women's Medical there. She started having babies. She wrote me to say that I should consider going there, but I stayed where I was. We lost touch with each other and then I ran into her in Stanley Park in Vancouver much later. She was unmistakably Saskia, her hair flaming like the vine maple trees. It must have been fall. I had some explaining to do that day since we had never openly talked about how I was Mary-Margaret, not Martin. Funny we always kept that sort of flirtatious way of being with each other even after we were both women again. I mean after I was a woman.

But back at medical school, I had to work hard to catch up when I got better and I had to work hard at my composure, with Hébert and the Dean both knowing my secret. Some days I thought they all knew. Or perhaps they were a bit stupid about sex. I'm sure there were rumours and that when the men got together, they laughed at me. I think a certain kind of woman could have pulled it off better. I was sure to seem eccentric whether I was dressed as a man or as a woman. I was never as eccentric as I seemed, either way.

I now believe Dr. Campbell knew the truth before I was sick, possibly from the beginning. I'm grateful to him for his openness, his discretion. Perhaps others sensed his protection and backed off. One of the men sang a song about women going to war -- sang it to tease me when I came into a room. But Dean Campbell was there in the room once when it happened and the man never sang that song again.

Yes, I now believe that eventually everyone at the university knew I was a woman, that they pretended not to know so they wouldn't have to do anything. And by "everyone" I mean the doctors who ran the school, the male medicos, those men who were one part Pope, one part unctuous storekeeper, rubbing their hands. How I hated those oily men, those men who were so careful of their power, so ambitious, so intense. But why did they let me pass? I have no answer. If only clarity would come like drops of rainwater on bare branches.

FOURTEEN

When I finished medical school, I got on a train headed west. I intended to go to Winnipeg and set up my practice. I went west as men have before me when they had to make a new life. It was all new; west was the way to go. I decided on Winnipeg because that's where a woman doctor, Sarah Blackmore had gone with her husband and she seemed to have made a useful life as a physician, treating ax wounds from fights and delivering the odd baby. So I heard when I went to that talk on women doctors. That was a detail that stayed with

The Modern Age

me somehow, stayed in my imagination. But when the train stopped in Winnipeg, I got out and walked around and then got back on. I decided it wasn't far enough west.

When I got on the train in Montreal, I packed my two suits in a suitcase and intended to go to Winnipeg as a man. I couldn't imagine setting up practice as a woman. I admit I hadn't really thought it out. I wasn't really operating from the thinking part of me at that time. Anyway, when I got off the train in Winnipeg, there was a store with a mannequin in the window, a woman's figure, curved like a woman, dressed as a woman in a grey twill skirt, slightly flared below the knee and a simple white blouse of cotton or linen. They were selling ready-made women's clothes, unusual at that time. I went in and bought a skirt and a blouse and jacket quickly, casually, without checking sizes, just by eye. Then I rushed back and made it back on the train before it left.

Out of breath in my compartment, the lurch of the train as it started to move was like the lurch of my heart. I closed my eyes as we slowly pulled out of the station, thinking I should have bought a hat too, and then just sat listening to the pounding of my heart. When I opened my eyes again, the train was up to speed and the window was full of fast-moving grass and sky. I stood to lock the compartment door and pulled down the blinds onto the corridor. I left open the sky window. Then, standing and bracing my knees against the lurching of the train, I took off my suit jacket and folded it carefully on the seat. I removed my tie and folded it on top of the suit jacket. I undid my cufflinks and the buttons of my shirt, took that off, and hung it on the back of the compartment door. Then I undid the scarf to loose my breasts. I looked at myself in the small mirror above the tiny sink, something I hadn't really done in a long time. I just looked; I didn't really think anything, just took in: breasts, short hair, waist, skin. Is it possible I'd fooled myself too? Then I took off my boots and pants and sat naked on the prickly grey plush of the train seat with my breasts free, my hands loose in my lap above the fur of curly hair, while brilliant sunshine and rolling prairie rushed by outside. I sat with my breasts free wondering at the strangeness of it all. Ever since that day I've been a freer person, less concerned with how things look, with keeping up appearances.

I changed from man to woman in my compartment on the train between Winnipeg and Banff, or between lunch and dinner. Actually Winnipeg to Banff takes longer than that, but that's how it felt. I got off the train in Banff as a woman and walked the platform as a woman, looking at mountains. Once again, I was dependent on the discretion of a public person, in this case the porter, who'd seen me come on as a man and saw me leave as a woman. My hair was very short still; I had it cut just before I left. But I wound the lavender scarf that had bound my breasts around my head and kept my hair covered until it grew back to a womanly length.

I arrived in Vancouver, then a rather rough and muddy little town, as a woman. I was tired of the masquerade. I set up practice as a woman. I thought of forging my medical papers and adding a female name but I didn't. I set up practice as Dr. Martin Howard, a woman. I applied to St. Paul's Hospital as Dr. Martin Howard. I had Dr. Martin Howard written in gold letters on the glass window of my second floor office on Georgia Street. Occasionally someone asked me whether Martin was a woman's name and I said, "No, my first name is Mary-Margaret", but I answered to either. I encountered the usual amount of prejudice and hostility for being a woman doing something unusual, but I seemed to have developed some degree of equanimity. It didn't bother me as much as I thought it would, or perhaps thought it should. Looking back, I'm amazed at what I took with a small smile.

Vancouver was a charming boomtown growing up in the wilderness. It had plank sidewalks in most places, muddy roads and a grand Opera House. Carbon arc lamps, electric streetcars, and the occasional bear sighting. It looked cosmopolitan on Hastings Street with its canvas awnings, sidewalk, and power poles, men in suits with their black hats and women in blouses with the puffed sleeves and high collars

The Modern Age

of the time pushing English prams. But the wilderness was just off the end of the sidewalk. Capilano water came in pipes to the houses. Electricity came in wires from Buntzen Lake.

It was summer when I arrived to a spectacular view of Coal Harbour with the misted mountains of the North Shore across the water. Those mountains became my touchstone. I could see them from my office windows, even later when I moved into the new Georgia Medical Dental building, mountains filling the window, changing in different lights and seasons, now with clouds like a Chinese painting, now with fresh snow on the trees, now close and now distant.

It took a while to get my practice going so I had time on my hands that summer. I hiked down to English Bay and bathed among the rocks there. It was extremely pleasant. I wasn't too worried about my loneliness. I went to Woodward's Department Store and bought myself a bathing costume, which covered me from the neck down, complete with sandals. I savoured being a woman among women; we bathed on the other side of the big rock from the men. Later the Women's Christian Temperance Union got all huffed about a girl who went in without her stockings and the members wrote to the newspaper. The girl won a libel case against them and got damages. I must say the bathing costume itched. I went back to Woodward's to buy a parasol for my bathing expeditions. The next summer they cleared the rocks away.

The place was raw and new. When I arrived, Vancouver was in the middle of a boom. I stayed in one of the small hotels that are now on Skid Row; then it was fine. The room was small and clean and I stayed for almost a year until my money came in. There were hundreds of real estate agents eager to show me around. But there was an ugly side. In 1907 when the recession came on, that part came squishing to the surface. The thugs in the Asian Exclusion League got active and staged riots in the Chinese area, breaking windows. Then came harsh laws against Asian immigration. These hatreds were like the loose planks squirting muddy water up on your skirts through the cracks when a weight passed over. I loved the place in the summer but in the winter it was mud everywhere. Mud on everything.

I set up my practice in a small office downtown on Georgia Street. I went in to the Dawson Hardware Store and walked between the rows of lawn mowers, birdcages, teapots, Bissels carpet sweepers, and wire waste paper baskets. There I bought the glass-fronted cabinets in which I kept my tools and instruments, and which are now here in my apartment in Kerrisdale, gleaming in the morning sun and holding an innocuous bunch of china and knickknacks.

It was intensely pleasurable to me to walk into the office in the morning and see this place I had produced with my own effort: the dark wood desk where I wrote prescriptions, the dark chairs, the examining table where pregnant women surrendered to my examinations, the window with its frosted glass, the locked cabinet with its medicines, the books on the shelf. I cleaned the office myself and at first I did my own bookkeeping and billing.

It took a while to get the practice set up. For a while I was quite strapped for money. My orchid money was pretty much gone and I wasn't bringing much in. But Vancouver quadrupled its population between 1901 and 1911 so I was needed, and I soon had a full roster of patients, despite being a woman. My patients were mostly women and children. I delivered babies and looked after them as they grew.

A year after I arrived, I came into my trust fund. I decided to buy a house for myself, to settle in Vancouver. Having looked about, I chose a small house out in the new neighbourhood of Kerrisdale near the Canadian Pacific Railway gardens where they grew the flowers and vegetables you got on the trains and the big hotels. It was a long way to go every day downtown to my office, to the hospital, or to the homes of my patients who were mostly in the West End. I drove my own buggy in all weathers and at all times of the day and night, and I was one of the first in the city, maybe the tenth or eleventh, to get a motor car. It would have been easier to settle in Kitsilano, which was serviced by the streetcar then, but I was immensely satisfied with myself and with my life. I came home at the end of the day to my own little house. It was more of a cottage than a house. I had my own large garden with vegetables and fruit trees and flowers, which I had a man to build and tend. I had a loyal housekeeper who kept meals warm for me. I had a big pile of sawdust in the basement, which I shoveled onto the fire myself. It amazed me to own windows, chairs, things all around, a large gilt mirror over the fireplace reflecting the open door, a tilting mirror on the dressing table with curved legs. I was perhaps too proud of my possessions and now couldn't give a fig for them.

Then in 1910 or 1911 women property owners were allowed to vote in the city of Vancouver and I was very satisfied to be able to do that too.

It turns out I was lucky to have bought that house when I did. I'd left the bulk of my money with Cornelius to manage and he lost it all in the 1907 stock market crash. There was nothing left. I never did find out what he'd actually done with it, but I was assured quite reliably that it was completely gone. So I was a wealthy woman, a woman of means, for approximately two years and all I ever got out of it was a house. But that was plenty.

And the mention of 1907 brings me back to the subject, to Zoë who was lost to me for those years of medical school and setting up my practice. For quite a while now I've managed to keep from writing about the real thing that's bothering me. I've written about my tragic love affair with Hugo, about medical school, about dressing as a man, about charming Vancouver. And I'm nowhere closer to what I wanted to figure out. What amazes me is the mind's capacity for stalling and blocking byways and putting up a lot of confetti to keep from looking at the real thing. Red lipstick over greedy lips. Why am I so afraid?

FIFTEEN

Zoë then:

She has a mole on her right collarbone at the hollow. But anyone who sat across from her at a dinner party could tell you that. What kind of mother was she? A mother who would leave her child. A mother who would leave her child is desperate. She didn't leave a note. She left him to me but I was unable to keep him with me.

She was. She was a good mother. She loved Morgan fiercely, properly, as any mother would. A snake on the path. Lifted him up, his long legs dangling. A wasp's nest. Fierce in the face of danger. She couldn't protect him from her own demons. He learned to be quiet on bad days, just as Zoë learned to be quiet on her mother's bad days. How we can't do anything to protect each other from this pain. What makes me think I can be objective about Zoë? Zoë pushing Morgan in the pram along the wooden sidewalks.

She was still so young. Only twenty-four when she died. So much she could have done with her life. To have seen Morgan grow up and become this ordinary sweet man. She had to forgo that because…because…

But who am I to judge since I left her from the time she was twelve 'til she was seventeen. Just walked out of her life and I owed her something too. Intimate friends, sister-niece for the first twelve years and then gone.

How she looked when I left: flickering on the edge of womanhood. Pushing me away, becoming independent. Funny, doing imitations. Here's Jim the gardener…his slow walk down the garden. Here's Cornelius…rocking on his toes, pursing his lips, twinkling. Doing Cornelius for Susannah; taking Susannah to the edge of heresy about her marriage, to the edge of admitting it was awful. She was animated, doing imitations, and then suddenly flat, turning away, right out of energy.

Fighting over the camera, hissing, perhaps a bit spoiled. Wrinkling her nose at me. Rolling her eyes. Mobile, athletic, barefoot in summer.

Barefoot as a woman in our Kerrisdale garden, with Morgan on her hip, shocking the neighbours.

Standing barefoot on my shoes when she was little, linking my hands under her arms so that I could walk with her on my feet.

Rolling her eyes at Cornelius stomping, heavy-footed overhead.

The Modern Age

I wasn't afraid of her, but some people were because her will was so fierce and her intentions so direct. Who was afraid of her? Cornelius? Susannah?

Her toys: a wind-up soldier, ceramic doll with pink taffeta dress, tattered and dirty. Set of tiny teacups. She would have me sit and drink tea with her. Her postcards. Croquet.

Her photographs, with the brownie camera and later with better cameras. Her painting of course, always.

Five years can pass in a minute. Five years in my practice passed just like that. Children that I delivered grew into human beings and moved on. But five years in a child's body can take a very long time. Five years in a lonely child's body. Zoë alone in her body for five years when I ran away. Maybe that's why she got pregnant.

What makes you mad about her? That she went away.

Talking to Morgan about his mother Zoë was taboo most of the time. I never had the courage to do it. Penny insisted. She wanted to know. "Tell me about my grandmother." But I didn't know enough. Maybe she will solve the mysteries.

Am I afraid? Is this lump that I feel in my chest fear? Before you can be honest, you have to understand. To understand you have to be not afraid to look. It's almost impossible.

I guess I've been hoping that if I keep writing down the facts, or what I think are the facts, I'll be able to see the truth myself. But I feel far from it right now.

These are the facts:

In 1906, Zoë was wild, in love with a truly unsuitable man, a married man in London. I conspired with Cornelius to separate them. She came to me in Vancouver. She was pregnant. I tried to talk her into an abortion. She would not have one. In 1907 there was a stock market crash. Cornelius killed himself. All the money was gone, including Zoë's and mine. Morgan was born.

The Modern Age

Something happened to Zoë. What was it? I puzzle and puzzle over that question. One damn thing after another. When she came out to Vancouver. Thin shoulders. Dark blonde hair, dark eyes. She carried the baby in front like a ball. She was an old seventeen. Sophisticated in that small town atmosphere. She made waves. She rebuffed the men. She was aloof.

She brought a trunk full of art supplies – good paper, paints, canvas. She walked through my small house assessing rooms for their light qualities. She settled in the upstairs attic and hired a man to come and finish it with a new window to the north. She hung the short walls under the sloping ceilings with her bright pictures, had a couch hauled up the narrow stairs, and made pillows with unusual fabrics. It was different in every way, but reminded me somehow of Hugo's room in London.

On a good day, she would spend a great deal of time in that room, and when I came home from work would call me up to see what she'd been doing. She was not secretive about her painting and had no superstitions about showing it to me. She signed her paintings Zoë Jones and sold some of them to friends. In the eight years or so she lived with me there, she painted about thirty pictures. She had one show, organized by a women's club, at an improvised art gallery on Hastings Street.

She suffered the bad taste of the small town without saying anything. Few people liked her paintings, or understood them. One sunny Saturday afternoon, we stood in the storefront gallery just out of sight of passers-by. Some people, mostly women, would stop and look, poker-faced or frowning. One older woman came back twice while we stood there to look at the melting landscape on an easel in the window. Perhaps it reminded her of something. That seemed to satisfy Zoë and she moved away from her scrutiny of the street and packed up her bag to go home to Morgan.

She had been influenced by the Impressionists, I think, and painted mundane subjects that seemed to glow with light – cups, scissors, lemons. Perhaps they were a little crudely rendered. She never had a drawing lesson as far as I know. I don't know anything about art and I really don't know whether the paintings were good or not. I liked them very much. Most of the paintings belong to Morgan and his daughters now, but I still have three here in my apartment.

One hangs where I can see it from my bed and is a self-portrait. Perhaps you can see what we might now call mental illness. She has painted herself as a crone, old and poor, and alone on a street that is very dark with circles of light meandering into the distance behind her grey head. At first the painting seems disturbing and dark, but I have always wanted it nearby. Lately I think there has been something new welling up through the darkness. Maybe in the pools of light. When I am near sleep and the room is lit only by the street light outside my window, the painting seems to move. Perhaps I am hallucinating as I get closer to the end here but I would swear that it is changing. What is it welling up in the circles of light?

In the spring of 1907 Zoë arrived on the same day as the telegram from Cornelius announcing her disappearance. She was wearing an elaborate black dress and a gold wedding ring, claiming to be a widow. Wearing widowhood: "We were married quietly in Derbyshire. He died of fever." "He died in a gun battle with highway robbers," she told someone later. "He lived in a big house in Derbyshire." Married secretly because of Cornelius. So she said.

I came to the conclusion from the sketchy details that she had only met this man, this husband, once or twice, in strictly social situations, and he wasn't the father of her child after all, my dear Morgan. I heard later from Susannah, who knew the family, that he died in 1914 at the first Battle of the Marne with the British Expeditionary Force. Like Hugo.

Much later I went to Somerset House in London and looked up the details of this man's life, bound in the big leather books row on row with all the other lives. He was already married in 1906 when Zoë knew him, although she may not have known that.

The Modern Age

But suddenly Zoë was with me. She arrived on the same day as Cornelius's frantic long telegram. I don't know what took him so long to get in touch with me. Zoë had told him something to distract him from her real purposes and her real dilemma -- that she was staying with someone in the country. His telegram was preemptory, harsh, accusatory, and presumptuous: Your responsibility now Stop.

I spent three dark hours trying to figure this out while I worked away with my patients, looking into the smooth and wrinkled bodies with their cross hatched textures, feeling their dry feet, and listening to their little drumbeats and rattles. When I finally got a moment to sit and think, it came to me that what he meant was that she was pregnant. And so she was.

But then she was there. She just appeared in my office, having traveled across the Atlantic, then by train across the country, alone. She arrived all dressed in black, posing as a widow. She was seventeen. I hadn't been back to London; I hadn't seen her for five years. She'd become a woman: breasts, waist, hips and something in the eyes. She was completely herself, vibrant, alive. I didn't recognize her at first. I couldn't believe it. I knew her right away. I opened my arms and she stepped into them. I could smell her hair, feel her curves, her body. She was pregnant.

I'm not shy about the body. I was not shy with her. I asked, not the first night, but the next day, and she didn't deny it. How did I know that the black widow's weeds were a fraud? And there was something else.

You hardly noticed at first with the distraction of the big hair around her face, but in the daylight I could see she had a long scar along her cheekbone. Susannah had written me about this peculiar church Zoë had been involved with, something High Anglican with a theosophist strain. Susannah said that Zoë had been dancing in the incense and the bowl exploded in her face. At breakfast in my sunny dining room, half a world away, I took her hands in mine, her hands bigger than mine now. She had shiny burn scars on the palms and a long scar along her cheekbone where a shard of hot pottery flew up and cut her. She said, "The minister's voice was beautiful. He lost his voice, jumped over the communion rail, almost fell, and laughed. I laughed. The air was filled with this joyous sound." I said, "But there were scars."

What does that mean? Dance in the incense. The smoke coming up in her face, making her feel dizzy, her legs and feet bare under the flowing dress. Bare feet cold on the tiles of the narthex. The minister must have been in love with her. I came to the conclusion that he was not the father either.

The third day she was there, and for the third time I heard her shuffling down the yellow hallway with the morning sun making squares of light along the wall and then came upon her throwing up in the bathroom, I realized I had to face the fact that she was pregnant. What did I do? Why I picked a fight with her of course. I stood outside the bathroom with my arms crossed and picked a fight. And I was late for the office and kept my patients waiting an hour or more, which I prided myself on never doing.

I don't want to write about abortion. People get so upset. I get upset. However I try to tell this part of Zoë's story, I am going to be misunderstood. Even saying merely that it's a complicated issue will bring brimstone on my head. I would rather not get into it at all even though my starting premise here has been that I am too old to care what anyone thinks and likely dead by the time anyone reads this anyway. But abortion is the subject I must write about because it was this question that brought a fatal chill between Zoë and me.

As a medical person, of course, I support abortion and would hope that it would be legalized some day soon. I need hardly sketch the vile circumstances into which pregnancy has put so many women. I saw it daily in my practice. The sorrow of women apparently decreed by a vicious angry God since the Garden of Eden. I don't buy it. I was, and am, repulsed by those who set out to profit from the sorrow of women and often enough left them worse off, sick, dying, bleeding. I had several prostitutes among my patients and grew to understand some of the sorrows that drove them to do what they did. Sally and Sue,

The Modern Age

(they didn't use their real names because no matter how degraded their families and the actions of their fathers and brothers, they still felt shame). They came from small towns to Vancouver and hid their shame under bravado. There's a whole book I could write about that, a book of sermons, but I have no time. I performed abortions when it was medically indicated, without fuss and without undue extra charge. I do hope I won't be arrested at this late day should I be wrong about how near I am to death. Now, in this age of the Beatles, I think not.

Zoë's situation seemed to indicate abortion. Seventeen years old, pregnant by a married man, who, although willing to support her financially apparently, though I personally doubted it, was not able to leave his wife. I put it to her forcefully.

I was not willing to perform an abortion on my own beloved niece, but I knew that I could find someone good to do it and I told her as much. Her reaction surprised me.

"You are the coldest person I have ever met in my life."

I didn't think of myself as cold. I was just trying to think things through properly and make the right decisions. Now of course I wouldn't have my dear boy Morgan if she hadn't won. Or I suppose my nieces Penny and Sarah who come by to play Beatles songs which is how I know it is the age of the Beatles. That makes Zoë right I suppose. And the anti-abortionists would say "Aha!" But what about Zoë and Zoë's life? Would she still be alive, my companion in aging? With another family, not Morgan, but someone like him?

She raged through it. She was like an electrical device which emotion caused to come alive and glow. She knew things I did not think it was possible to know. She dreamed of the unborn child and dreamed his name, dreamed he was walking around speaking to her. She believed her lover would come to her.

And now, almost sixty years later, I still wonder, who was the father of that child, that is Morgan's father and the girls' grandfather?

I yelled at Zoë, "I forbid you to go through with this

The Modern Age

pregnancy." She dug in and looked back at me with that stubborn look, then patted my arm, so she was comforting me like a replaying of some childhood thing we did. I yell, she pats my arm. Where do these patterns come from?

Then I took her to see Mrs. Alice Berry, a woman I admired, who was becoming a friend of mine. She'd set up a company with Mr. L.D. Taylor (who she later married) to purchase The World newspaper, and she was the managing director. She lived down on Robson Street, in a nice house with a beautiful garden, where we sat and had tea in the early spring sunshine. He was there too, her Mr. Taylor, quite leftish and pro-suffrage, outspoken. I hoped that Mrs. Berry would impress Zoë as she'd impressed me and persuade her to give up the baby. I telephoned Mrs. Berry beforehand to explain, then left them alone together. But nothing would persuade her. Of course I am so glad now, Morgan, dear.

Now today is another rainy day and windy, this day dark and wet. Leaves still green and yellow cling to the trees. Suddenly, a memory: Zoë arguing with Hugo about the orchids. "You should let them just grow," she said. "They're beautiful but you should leave them alone. They don't like it here. They want to be alive, not dying here in a foreign country."

Hugo said, "This isn't a foreign country. This is England." In some ways that was an uncharacteristically stupid remark for him to make. In other ways it was exactly the stupid place in the middle of his forehead. "This is England." Zoë was not yet eleven at the time.

So she went ahead with the pregnancy and gave up the widow's weeds after a month, having established she was Mrs. Ronald Montgomery-Jones, which she dropped down to Jones to honour the simplicity of the New World.

Then we had a few months of pleasant, almost idyllic, life. The nausea passed. I accepted the pregnancy and shrugged off the looks of neighbours. She was happy again. She took up the running of my house, but did it by befriending my

The Modern Age

housekeeper and keeping company with her. She had meals ready for me when I came home and spent her own money, which came regularly from Cornelius, on pretty things for my house: an Irish lace tablecloth, a Persian carpet, which I still have, an upright piano. On weekends we took the streetcar and paddled in the water at Greer's Beach or rode the boat to the North Shore where we hiked and picnicked in the woods. We even had a social life, going to dinners and tea parties at the homes of the new society growing here in Vancouver. We weren't together the way we were before because we weren't children any more, but we knew each other well and we were easy with one another. Once again it seemed there were no grown-ups around. We were happy to take care of each other.

Zoë got bigger. She settled down into her body. We set up a room for the baby. We would have called it Katherine Elizabeth for our two mothers if it had been a girl. We didn't even discuss boys' names. Summer passed. The rains came, the cedars dripped darkly, and the streets turned muddy again. She stayed home and let the housekeeper do the shopping. But she was energetic. She was painting the nursery white when the telegrams started coming.

The first telegram said there had been a financial panic. We shrugged.

The second said, All Money Gone or perhaps Money All Gone. We laughed. "Thank heavens for the telegraph or we wouldn't know," we joked. "Ah the Modern Age."

But we really didn't understand. The 1907 Financial Panic was the most severe ever up to that time. It started with rumours of problems at Knickerbocker Trust. The rumours reached the Rockefellers and Vanderbilts at the Jekyll Island Club and J.P. Morgan rushed back to New York to raise enough money to save the situation. But not for us. Men like George Westinghouse lost control of their companies. Automobile firms went under. There were bank failures. Theodore Roosevelt was blamed. Cornelius had been caught up in the frenzy of speculation that started in about 1901 with electrification, radio waves, and the new age. But his investing got wild and he was caught. We were caught.

My money had been somewhat abstract to me, first used as a control on my actions and denied me, then freed by law when I didn't need it anymore, when I was making a comfortable living from my practice. I bought my house with the trust money, but since then I had been living quite simply on my earnings as a doctor. And, except for a time during the thirties when things got a bit testy, would continue to do so. I believed in myself and my ability to support myself even if it was based on the illusions developed while growing orchids. We didn't understand that it meant what it said, all money gone, my money, Zoë's money, all gone.

The third telegram was from Susannah and said: Cornelius dead. Stop. Shooting accident. Stop. Do not come. Stop.

Now my memory is going. But it is strangely alert and competent in some brightly lit areas, discovering details I didn't see at the time. It gives me a picture of Zoë the evening we got the telegram about Cornelius, sitting in our little living room by the fire, her face icy and white, stroking the silky terrier on her lap, under her pregnant belly, the terrier we'd recently brought in from Australia. His coat was glossy blue gray and tan, shining in the firelight and her hands were stroking rhythmically. Now, in memory, I want to write the word sorrow, stroking rhythmically with great sorrow, the coat of the silky dog we called Jim because he looked at us with the patient attention of the gardener at Holland Street in London. Now I wonder, what was Cornelius to Zoë? "I'm glad he's dead," she said softly and I thought she was bitter about the money.

SIXTEEN

So November 19, 1907, the night we heard about Cornelius, was the night Morgan was born. It was a quick birth too. I heard Zoë make a funny sound at about 10:30. At first I thought she was sleep talking, as she sometimes did, and almost went back to sleep. But I thought better of it and forced myself up. She was in the bathroom and her water had broken. I had never seen poor Zoë look so nonplussed. She was standing in her yellow nightgown all wet, with her hands dropped at her sides. I helped her clean up and got her back to her room then I telephoned her doctor, Dr. Clarke. It was an awful night to call someone out, rainy and blowing, but he said he was on his way. The roads were muddy too from six days of steady rain. She went into labour, with her first contraction about midnight and the baby was born at 1:37 before my colleague could get there. I lifted the baby out, held him up to the light, smacked him for his first breath, cut the cord, washed him, put him to his mother's breast, and cleaned up afterwards. That was you Morgan, born with that kind of quick stubborn determination that has characterized your whole life. Bullheaded and bothersome, convinced of your right to be there. Well fine, we were very glad of you. She, at least, had never wavered in her desire to see you into the world.

We were very glad of Morgan, named for J.P. because of the money being lost that night. And then we were raising you. Like those pictures I saw on television the other day of orchids unfolding in time lapse, you grew: a baby, a toddler, a child, then seven years old. Now a man of fifty-eight with your grey hairs and wrinkles.

The next seven years slipped by with the burble of child talk, ripples of concern about childhood fevers and bumps, small dissensions and irritations about daily life. It was a good time.

The city grew. Our neighbourhood blossomed. We changed from an outpost in the wilderness to a real place. By 1910, the streetcar went along Cambie and out Forty-first almost to my front door. I was settled as a family physician and more or less accepted. I knew about the Bell-Irvings and Rogers, the high society of Vancouver, but was not part of it. Zoë and I were more of the middle society, the people who knew the high society of that small town. But for a brief time we did get swept up into the new high society in a surge of money that came and went just before the war.

Von Alvensleben, as we called him -- I can't remember ever hearing his first name -- arrived in Vancouver in 1904, penniless. He got onto the Vancouver Stock Exchange in 1907 and did very well, bought a twenty-acre Kerrisdale estate, down the hill off Forty-first. There he led the "gay life", throwing big dinners, garden parties, tea parties. I read about him in the newspaper.

    One day he tripped on Georgia Street, right outside my office building. His chauffeur brought him up and I dressed a nasty leg wound he got from falling across a piece of scrap metal. He claimed it was fate, that he'd been looking for a doctor. He put himself in my hands medically. He had some liver problems because he drank too much and I advised him to stop but he didn't, though he claimed to admire my medical skills and at parties told the story of how we met. For a little over two years, Zoë and I went often to his parties at the Kerrisdale mansion, sometimes once a week, sometimes once a month. I didn't really enjoy the parties themselves but hoped that by being sociable, Zoë would meet someone and be happier. Or maybe I didn't hope that at all. She didn't meet anyone. In retrospect I think I was happy enough at the time to have her and the boy to look after and would have been lost if she married and moved the boy away. But lost I was anyway as it turned out. Is it possible that my memory of that happy time is totally wrong and that she was muffled and sheltering me from this darkness that broke through when the War started? I don't know.

    Anyway, Von Alvensleben was wiped out in the next market crash of 1913, he left Vancouver, and his house went dark. The gossip was that his property in the U.S. was seized in 1914 and he was declared an enemy alien.

    I saw the doctor today and I have breast cancer. He wouldn't say how long I have but I know I don't feel too well. With great trepidation I told Morgan when he came by for tea. He went completely pale and just sat there holding his hands in his lap. I expected him to start fussing again, but he didn't.

Such a little life, so short. But somehow it filled up the edges of everything. Now I've filled these pages with thoughts and squabbles about it all, I look back with some equanimity and think it wasn't too bad. It had its moments. I am very tired now and think I might sleep.

Three days since I sat here and wrote. Wandering around the apartment while it rained outside and the dog followed me with his eyes. Standing in the doorway while he did his business in the dark. It was a black hole I was covering up with my chatter of parties and streetcars. I went down the black hole last night. No sleep until about four, then fitful dozing. My eyes in the mirror this morning are hollow and dark.

All along I've been presenting those years, and even thinking of them, as something like "the happiest years of our lives", meaning for both me and Zoë, and Morgan too I guess. But I have remembered now: a time when Morgan was four and Zoë took ill. Illness like a dark shadow came across my life again and I'd completely forgotten. This cancer diagnosis has perhaps cleared the fog a bit? I don't know.

Zoë always wore bright colours, turquoise blue with bright red velvet piping. Or red stockings with an orange skirt. She looked Japanese one day, German in lederhosen the next. Her body was a work of art, a changing window display, as unsettled as the leaves in fall, sometimes even quite ugly. Maybe that's how I've preserved this unreliable memory of happiness, by remembering her lovely clothes. She wore shocking blue, her face bare, for no-one wore make-up then, her beauty bare to the world. She was unafraid and said that by how she dressed. I remember particularly a short dark grey jacket with silk grosgrain tucked at the waist and stitched in geometric lines across the skirt. As unsettled as the sea and as cold.

And then she was sick. She developed a cough, which

wouldn't go away. A ring of copper against copper. I was reminded of something, I wasn't sure what. The child was four. Zoë began to weep uncontrollably and then developed this dry cough, as though she was trying to dislodge something from her throat. Weeping and then coughing dryly, holding the boy too close, watching him too closely. Staying close to home, no fun any more.

I just don't want to write about this.

Let's say: Zoë got sick, she was unwell, she died. I am now confused about what happened. I feel my mental capacities have dimmed in the relatively short time I've been writing this. I started in the New Year and it's June already. Or maybe it feels like my mind has dimmed but it's just this not wanting to know like a heavy blanket on the head. Suffocating really.

My strong will is what has served me well all my life. I have returned to this after another several days of pacing, by will, by ignoring Morgan's anxious phone calls and visits. I have completely put him off by a story about what the doctor says. I'm old. Cancer does not move swiftly in the old. This is what the doctor said. Morgan is very frightened

What is it I'm so confused about? First what triggered it? It? A bout of what I called hysteria, or was diagnosed as hysteria. She developed a dry unproductive cough. She cried. She couldn't sleep. She startled easily.

I am using my will to dig back into the hard dirt of that time. My shovel rings on rock. I remember this: sitting in my friend Alice Berry's garden on Robson Street, Morgan coming and going, eating cherries. Zoë was at home in a dark room. Now I remember telling Alice how worried I was. She said, "Have you read this man Freud?" Of course I'd known of the doctor from Vienna and his outrageous theories about sex. Perhaps I looked shocked. She said something conciliatory. "I'm not saying anything about Zoë. I'm sure she's fine." And

The Modern Age

then, "You should look into it, maybe." Alice always got to the point. She and her husband ran a hardheaded business, a newspaper, and they owned a sawmill.

So I did look into it. I sent for the books. I read about Dora. I read about her loss of voice, her cough, her hysteria. It all seemed to fit Zoë. I read how poor Dora had both electrical and hydropathic treatment. How she wet the bed at six or seven and at 12 developed the cough and migraines. How she had gastric pains, vaginal discharge, irregular periods and at sixteen, fever and abdominal pain. How something happened to her at the age of eight. But what? Her sexuality changed. Honestly I can't remember now what the doctor wrote, just that poor old Dora had such a rough time of it. Her weary trek from doctor to doctor, her nymphomania. That part didn't seem to fit Zoë now but I'd seen that myself in a patient, a prostitute. And now, looking back on Cornelius's worried letters, perhaps it was nymphomania he was writing about when she was seventeen and wild in London.

And I read on about hysteria. Men stated their hypotheses as absolute certainties. Hysteria means "wandering uterus". These were thought to be causes of hysteria: earthquake, lightning, excitation of sense organs, fever, disease, infection, diabetes, lead poison, alcohol, hemorrhage, diarrhea, overwork, too much sexual activity, excessive physical or mental labour, fatigue, parental maltreatment, the idle life of the rich, the poverty of the poor. And then "Nearly all women are said to be somewhat hysterical."

Here's one of the books I read at the time, still on my dusty shelves: Samuel Wilks' Lectures on Diseases of the Nervous System: "When not doing work that belongs to them such as the raising of children, domestic avocations, and the like... (women's) superfluous energies, having no outlet, the whole system becomes disordered and hysteric symptoms ensue." That was 1878, just thirty-three years earlier.

Freud described the hysteric cough: a harsh loud monotonous bleat or bark, hollow or metallic, repeated for

The Modern Age

hours with no expectoration. Like Zoë. Leaving Sunday service at St. Mary's church in the middle of the sermon because it wouldn't stop. She was so unhappy. So I diagnosed her: hysteric. But doctors were torturing hysterics: putting hot irons to their thin spines, tubes in their rectums, performing ovarectemies, cauterizing clitorises. I was attracted to Dr. Freud's talking cure. Was there a way that was more humane? There were no doctors in Vancouver doing that kind of work at the time. So I proposed we travel to Toronto to see Dr. Ernest Jones, said to be an associate and friend of Dr. Freud's. She shrugged and we went.

I'd forgotten all of this. Now I remember being on the train with her and the boy, the rails beating out their rhythm: there's nothing I can do. There's nothing I can do. We sat to large meals in the plush dining car, pretending to be normal. Zoë played with her food to make it look like she'd eaten. We swayed up and down the train, leading the child. Or she carried him heavy on her hip, his legs hanging down. We looked out the window at mountains, prairies, rocks, lake, city, as the country rolled by outside. And all the while the rails beat out this rhythm: there's nothing I can do.

It seems bizarre to me now that I had so totally forgotten this part of our story. It's as though memory is capable of shrinking the unpleasant down to a dried little walnut in the bottom of the mind and pretending it is not there. Dust under the bed. If I weren't so old I'd want to know more about this. How could I "forget" this so well? Why am I able to remember it now with no stimulus except the act of will I exert by writing this?

Coming into Toronto, I took it as a good sign that I felt that I had been there before, that the red brick buildings, the English streets, were deeply familiar to me. Maybe that was a bad sign. What do I mean "a sign" anyway? Despite my best efforts, my years of trying to be a rational being, superstition creeps into my thinking.

We spent three months in Toronto, staying in rooms,

The Modern Age

until the money ran out and I had to go back to work. Zoë met with Dr. Jones three times a week, while I stayed with Morgan. On the train on the way home she said, "I feel like I'm in a coffin."

Two years later, Dr. Jones was involved in a terrible scandal. One of his former patients reported to the president of the University of Toronto that Dr. Jones had made sexual advances. She was supported in her allegations by her general practitioner. Dr. Jones claimed the woman doctor had had a lesbian relationship with his patient. But he also admitted paying blackmail money to the patient in order to keep her quiet. I tried to keep it all from Zoë but she found out. She said, "See?" holding out a long newspaper article, and walked out of the room. That "See?" rocks down the years to me. By then I could hardly ask her what she meant. Later I read a biography of Dr. Jones where Jones complained to Freud in his letters about feeling enormous fatigue as a result of this ordeal. I kept hoping the sun would come out. But it didn't.

The days passed, as they do. 1911, 1912, 1913. I believe she started to get a bit better. The sun did shine some days. The boy grew. I worked, delivered babies, set bones, and looked into throats and chests. She painted when she felt well enough.

In 1914, Susannah sent me money and begged me to come to England again to see her. I tried to take Zoë and Morgan but she said she was fine and would stay in Vancouver. She didn't want to go back there. She put herself out to appear competent and sunny while I booked my ticket and got ready to go. Morgan was to start school in the fall. Zoë said she'd be busy preparing him, buying clothes and supplies and starting him on his ABC's. Smaller and smaller on the train platform as the train pulled away. Turquoise coat smaller and smaller.

The enchanted summer of 1914. It will enter the songs that are sung about this time. The scraps of myth that survive will speak of this summer, a summer that stretched away into

The Modern Age

infinite time; that stands in for years of peace and prosperity, for what might have been. The summer of civilization. Well Morgan, you probably don't remember. The girls don't know. But you will hear that summer mentioned from time to time. The weather was glorious. The days shimmered. The nights were brilliant. What does it mean? Does weather know? Does weather reflect the mood of a time?

I spent that summer mostly in London and in a cottage in Cornwall with Susannah and her friends. Susannah was still living at the Holland Street house, barely living, still mourning Cornelius, but responsive to the sea, the light, the green of Cornwall. We walked on the cliffs and down by the sea. We talked about the weather. We read.

And there was a woman doctor from Paris who I'd gotten to know at a conference in Montreal in 1912 and I went across to meet her for a few weeks. It was lovely there. I was considered young again. Only 34 after all. She had a large group of friends, men and women. We all went out to the Bois de Bologne and sat under a canvas awning while an orchestra played the syncopated music that was the latest thing. We danced. We ate well. It was warm and sweet and a month later the war broke out.

In Paris I had a serious flirtation with a young French doctor, part of this jolly group. I don't even mention the man's name. I don't think I would recognize him if he walked down the street. But I remember the feel of him dancing, the feel of his jacket and the shape he made against me.

He kissed me under the trees in the Bois and it was lovely but there was never any possibility that something could come of it. I might have gone further with him, I rather wish I had, but there was no time, no place to be together. My life was back with my practice in Vancouver, in taking care of Zoë and Morgan. That was the last man to take an interest in me that way. It was not possible to be a womanly woman and a dignified physician in upright Vancouver. It took a European to see through that and the Europeans who came to Vancouver were not that subtle. It was one of the prices I paid for my ambition.

And why didn't I go further? What right do I have for this note of bitterness? Why did my ambition stop at this muddy town on the Pacific out on the edge of the New World? I don't know. I could say it was because of my responsibilities. I could say I was tired. I could say I was content. I could say all those things and they would be true.

After Paris, I went alone to Derbyshire at Tideswell in the Peak and stood under the church clock. I went to try to find my father's family's gravestones from the time before they came to Canada. Why I wrote this down I don't know, or why I saved it, but here it is in my desk, a bleak inscription off a gravestone from that place:

> George Bagshaw of Litton
> Died 85 years old 1806
> By Depth of snow, and stormy days
> He was bewildered in his way
> No mortal aid, did him come nigh
> Upon the snow he then did lie
> Helpless being worn out with strife.
> Death soon drew him of his life
> But hope he found a rotted way
>   To the regions of Eternal day.

I've fought so hard all my life against sentimentality. I suppose that is why it has such power over me, the power of what you fight against? I hate the lump in my throat I get when I read this. I hate the feeling welling up in me. And I am almost eighty-five, like poor George Bagshaw dying in the snow.

I talk about my will, and what I have achieved by the exertion of will, but what about Zoë? I can't imagine her drowning. She walked into the river fully dressed, wearing her beautiful dark cloak with the turquoise silk lining. I can't imagine the will it must take to drown yourself, eyes open, dazzled by the winter sun, water green and cold, cloak like a dark cloud above her, blown open by the wind. My Ophelia. I'm so frightened for her. Why did she? How did she keep herself from swimming? I know I would have swum, I so needy, so frightened, so hungry to be alive. Maybe she did swim, changed her mind, but too late, was taken anyway. How could she?

Why have I been avoiding the very plain truth that Cornelius was a monster? Why won't I come right out and say it? What is Zoë's story? It is very simple and the anguish does not belong to me at all. I said when I started writing this that I didn't care what people thought anymore. But obviously I do, or did. When will I reach the point of really not caring, and therefore be free to tell the truth? I realize now that it was Cornelius. Possibly he was Morgan's father? But actually I think not. I think now she truly didn't know who the father was. That she indulged in a little festival of promiscuity when she was sixteen, seventeen, for which I blame Cornelius regardless. But all this is a mystery and underlying it, the unsolvable mystery of what happened to Cornelius to make him this way, to make him brutal beyond belief, with the veneer of hale-fellow-well-met? And the question for you Penny, should you read this, as I expect you will since you are nosy beyond belief. The question, Penny, is what can be done about this chain of hurt that has been handed down to Morgan and to you and Sarah presumably? Are you going to do something about it? I wish I could have helped your mother more, I mean your grandmother. But I am a fool, an old fool, and really ready to call it quits

The foxgloves are ten feet tall now and bending down to whisper something to me. I cannot hear them so I say they are mute but now question whether the problem is me. My ears are not working right, clogged with anger and anxiety. Why am I so anxious all the time?

SEVENTEEN

Penny is home from England! She's coming here tonight. She says she has a letter for me that has been sealed and never delivered. The letter from H. Ryder, that's Hugo. She says it has a military censor's stamp dated September 15, 1914. That she found it in the house on Holland Street. Penny again! And a mysterious letter. From Hugo!

What is the story of this letter from Hugo? It must have arrived at the house in Holland St in 1914. Susannah must have realized who it was from and decided not to forward it to me. All these must haves, Hugo must have written it just before he died.

The Modern Age

So it lay in Susannah's letters which I didn't have the time or energy to read so just left in the box room on Holland Street for all these years. How many years? I went back to England for Susannah's dying in 1951 and it was my job to dismantle Holland Street. I don't remember the trunk. I didn't properly dismantle the house. Morgan said he might want it someday. I got an agent. The agent let the house. We got cheques semi-annually and did not have to think about it. And now Penny has found a hidden treasure. Hugo used to say, "I was a hidden treasure and I longed to be found." I don't know what he meant at all, it's just a phrase that sticks in my mind.

My belief is that we don't want to know. I don't want to know. That we can't know or we'd run screaming into the river. Like Zoë.

They say drowning is seductive, pleasurable. How do they know? This is a medical question surely and I should know. Water up the nose. Breathing in water. How quickly would darkness come? Lake or river. Currents. Wading in shoes slippers boots. Cold. Clothes clinging to her.

I was at a dinner party last night, a rare enough event now. There was a man there, a major, who everyone called The Major, and he was in costume, I mean uniform. Something about him, his puffed out chest, brought back Cornelius.

Cornelius, the master of bluff and bluster, the tickler, the storming wind. And what of Susannah? Perhaps I have underestimated her in all this.

Bang bang bang. Cornelius. No one else would dare to make that much noise. We all stop, look at each other (don't look at each other). Will someone let him in? Bang Bang. Zoë puts her head down to her drawing. Susannah gets up and goes to him. In a few minutes they come in together, followed by the maid with hot water for tea and two wet dogs. Cornelius and the dogs crowd up to the fire blocking it. I can feel the chill. A cat leaps out of a chair and away, followed briefly by one of the dogs. Cornelius chaffs his hands then suddenly wheels on me, "What's this about Greek?" I've been caught. "Why does a gel need Greek?"

"I want to go to medical school and become a doctor."

"A what?"

"A medical doctor."

"That's ridiculous."

Susannah hands him a cup of tea, managing him like a sheep dog, standing close to him and pushing slightly, sometimes barking, arguing. "We'll talk about it later dear. Did you have a good walk?"

Hugo said that he had been lost and was saved by nomads in the desert, and when you are brought back by nomads you are not the same.

Morgan took me for a drive today after Penny phoned. I steered him to the place by the river where his mother went in. Or where we suppose she went in. A sand beach on the north shore of the Fraser. She took my car for the day and they found it parked under the trees there. She left no letter, no reasoning. It was September 15, 1914, a few days after the First Battle of the Marne. Then, of course we didn't know it was the First Battle. Twelve thousand weary members of the British Expeditionary Force were killed, including Hugo. They had been retreating for ten days under German attack. I didn't know then that Hugo was there, was killed. He had been at Mons with the B.E.F. and was retreating to the Marne. I found out much later. Why was he even there? The man Zoë said was her husband was killed. He was driving military dispatches from Paris to the front. His car was hit and he was stranded in icy waters under a bridge held by Germans. Zoë did not know this when she died.

What happened to Morgan when she died? This time is sort of a haze for me. Perhaps this is the part I can not bear to look at. Morgan was taken from me. I was summonsed and appeared in Family Court. I did not take it seriously enough. I didn't even hire a lawyer. I thought we would just carry on,

The Modern Age

with the same nurse for him, me working; there would be no question, that anyone could see that Morgan was mine, as much as anyone's. But Kate's brother came to court with his wife, all the way from Windsor, Ontario and tore Morgan from me. That was Zoë's uncle. Who had never taken an interest in Zoë, never done anything for her. But he had a new wife and she couldn't have babies apparently, and wanted them, wanted Morgan. The court agreed with his eloquent, lying lawyer that it was better for a young boy to have a father, to have that manly, male influence. There was no father in sight with me. So he was taken. His things, wooden toys, his mother's drawings, his clothes, packed up in the trunk that had crossed the Atlantic twice with me and taken. And there was apparently nothing I could do. Zoë had left no will, nor any instructions. I suppose that she thought it would be obvious that I would take care of Morgan. Nothing could be more obvious. What could I do? Too late I hired a lawyer. He looked at the court papers and shrugged. Too late. Nothing to be done. I don't believe even he, my lawyer, thought I should raise a son alone. It wasn't done. The War was on. Many of the male doctors had left. There was a great need. I threw myself into work.

But this terrible loss of Zoë and of Morgan had an effect. I know it did. I think of myself as a good clinician. I admire a good clinician. A good clinician does not just prescribe something quickly. He (or she) listens to the body, touches it, uses the senses to reach a diagnosis. But with what did I touch my patients as I palpated their painful stomachs, bent my ear to their wheezing chests, or gently bent their arthritic arms and legs? Sorrow seeped into my hands. I touched them with sorrow, a stain of sorrow.

Now I remember that day in court. The blonde wood of the courthouse, sunlight through the tall windows, the rose coloured felt hat and dark wool coat that the young wife wore, the dark cloaks of the lawyers, their clubby camaraderie. The gruff friendliness of Zoë's uncle Harold and the shy prettiness of the young wife. Everyone acted as though everything was just normal, just business as usual. The hard bench where we all sat silently waiting for the decision. Morgan's calm little face as he shook my hand and went off stoically with his new family. Did he understand? How much did he understand? I was in shock. I did not scream with anger and outrage as I feel like doing now. He went off to live in Windsor and became a man away from me, sending me polite stoic Christmas cards over the years.

And how he came back. How he moved to Vancouver when he graduated from university and stayed, despite losing his job in the midst of the Depression, finding another, despite enticements to move to head office back east, to be closer to his second family, who raised him. How he opened his life to me, brought his daughters to me so that I became as a grandmother to them. We never spoke about Zoë, about how he was carried away from me, about how he came back. He just came back and made the assumption that we would see each other, that he would treat me as a dotty aunt who he cared about and for whom he cared. So I was there when the twins came home from the hospital and Linda put them, fresh and pink, arms waving, into my arms. How much did he tell her about us? I don't know. But somehow he stayed in my life. I am so grateful. And I say nothing to him, just fight him every step of the way to the nursing home and lie to him about the cancer.

So today I walked down on the little beach with Morgan trying to hold my arm. The sand was chalky with river mud. The sticks and logs on the river's edge were grey with it. I didn't tell Morgan why we were there, what this place meant. The Fraser is wide and flat here, at the mouth. It smells of the debris carried down from the wilderness. Boats of various kinds moved up and down, bucking the chop, some towing barges of logs, some with fishing gear on the decks. The sun was warm on our backs but it was cold in the wind. Morgan tried to get me to go back to the car.

The Modern Age

The war claimed nine million lives on both sides. Six thousand men killed every day. A whole generation of men crippled, unhinged. Anyway many have written about this, how this travesty of a war destroyed not only the men who might have been our husbands and lovers, but also our, perhaps naïve, but perhaps not, way of looking at the world as a place which was getting better, becoming modern, just, and right.

The First World War happened. That was the end of that, the end of a time of prosperity and expansion and growing freedom. Billions spent, millions killed. People expected it to happen. I've carried around this romantic notion that the whole world could have been different. But it was all laid out. They say there were German spies in England before the war. Back in 1887, Friedrich Engels predicted a world war of never before seen extent and intensity. The Thirty Years War condensed. Famine, epidemics, barbarization, desperation, chaos in trade, bankruptcy, collapse of the old states and their traditional wisdom. How will it end? Well he said it would end in the victory of the working class but I guess not. Killing Germans to save the world, our former friends and fellows.

And Zoë went into the river; she gave up believing that it could all come out somehow. And why I keep mentioning the Beatles, their sweet optimism ringing in my ears. The heavy darkness, the cloak being pulled down into the river, is forgotten. We really don't want to know. Optimism is a kind of rebirth, against all odds.

The 1918 influenza epidemic was my war. My own survival was a miracle, so many young people died. It is dim to me now, remembered through a haze of exhaustion and sorrow at the many losses. I can still close my eyes and open them four floors up looking south and west from the hospital. Like a dream. How did I get here? How will I survive? Closed my eyes, standing at the window looking into the setting sun. The sun still set beautifully into the ocean as though nothing at all had happened. My eyelids turned red as I fell into sleep and work again. I was often that tired. One day, a girl appeared at the end of the hallway bearing an armful of lilacs. The smell filled the hall as she came up to me. "Where is everyone?" She smiled in passing. I sat in a chair behind the sister's desk, stretched out my sore feet, crossed my arms across my chest and slept.

There was life after this death, this Zoë going. I remember things. In 1922 we started to drive on the right like the Americans and the younger people were doing the Charleston. In the twenties: the Woodward's beacon and the searchlight over the city, the Ku Klux Klan scare. In the 1920's I had a patient who was very ill with a heart condition who lived on the top of the Tenth Avenue hill in a small house on Tolmie Street. There was a plague of tent caterpillars. The streets were slippery with crushed caterpillar larvae. Sometimes the streetcars couldn't make it up the hill because the wheels slipped on them. In 1929 I moved my office into the new Georgia Medical Dental building.

Bobbed hair, Union Steamships, listening to the radio. Waking up in the morning to heavy fog because of the sawmill smoke. You don't see fog like that now. Or the soot on the houses. We had to wash curtains all the time. A colleague was insane with use of morphine for two years at age of 39 or 40. He overcame the habit himself without going to an asylum. I was involved in worthy causes. In 1922, Helen MacGill, who had set up a daycare for working women and worked vigorously on woman's suffrage, invited me to join the Vancouver Business and Professional Women's Club.

I weathered the Thirties, the Depression. People paid for their doctoring with produce from their gardens or a chicken. Some couldn't pay at all. We got by. The unemployed men had a Hunger March, which the police dispersed with clubs and horses. One heard about the work camps. Mayor Gerry McGeer read the riot act in Victory Square and there was the day the men occupied the Post Office and Art Gallery.

In 1944 I moved to one of the new apartments in Kerrisdale and gave Morgan and his young family my house. I'm still here in the same apartment. He's still in the house.

In the 1940's I was a member of the Air Raid

Precaution Organization, one of 10,000 volunteers in the city. We did public education about blackouts. For me the Second War was rationing, saving fabric, and daylight savings time. I heard about the Japanese removal, but it was distant. In the 1950's I joined the medical faculty at the university. I pursued my interest in restrictive clothing, and how women get inadequate exercise. We breathe from upper part of our chests instead of the deep diaphragmatic breathing that sustains health. I proposed a study on the effects of menstruation on women's activities and was turned down.

In 1945 the SS Greenhill Park blew up at pier B, killed 8 crew, and knocked out windows in the Post Office and the Marine Building, hurling material two miles away. I was at the hospital at the time and was called in to do emergency work. My line was almost totally births and children by then. The mangled bodies were unusual and vivid.

I honestly don't have the energy to remember all these things, though they were the warp and woof of what made up the fabric of my life.

There were other losses. A baby I had delivered died of scarlet fever and diphtheria at one year old. One of the babies, a girl, did not walk until she was 19 months old. She had large ankle and wrist joints and swelling of the knee. One of my young mothers had a baby at seventeen and in her nineteenth year died of tubercular meningitis. One woman told me her husband was on morphine and wanted intercourse more than once a day. She was worn out. "My husband says I am cold-blooded." I just tried to comfort her and sent her back to him. Maybe I shouldn't have. I tried to give the women who came to me some knowledge of sexual physiology, to be their friend in that.

EIGHTEEN

    Today I sat on a dirty log with my sensibly shod feet in the dusty sand of the river beach while Morgan hovered unwilling to put his good pants down on the gritty log. I've never cried, this whole dry life long. I am a person without tears. I sat and thought, regretted, imagined being under the water, pulled down. What is the drive to live? How did it so definitely leave Zoë? What has happened to her poor suffering soul? I imagine I shall know soon.

    The sun came out. Morgan pulled out a handkerchief to put on the log and sat down near me so I could smell him and feel his heat. I looked up at his face, his struggling to be good, to care for me. Sweet Morgan, the sweetest person I have ever known. The sun lit his hair, which is turning grey slowly. The sand rubs off my black pants easily and leaves a little sheen of grey. I find I can forgive Cornelius for sins real and imagined. And tonight I will have Hugo's letter, two hours.

"Well dear, I just don't understand," I said to Morgan. He grinned and shrugged.

The sun lit a ribbon of green on the water, a bright twist in the grey. I saw that there is a ribbon like that running through the chalky muck my life, call it joy.

Near the River Marne

September 9, 1914

Dearest Mary-Margaret,

A few moments ago I was awoken from a light sleep by a rooster crowing, a strange sound in this place, a sound that brings to mind country mornings and a peace that I'm afraid we took rather for granted. Today will be difficult. The hillside across from me is turning from grey to green as the light grows. Soon it will turn grey again no doubt with the clouds of German soldiers we expect. You probably don't know that I am a Captain in the British Expeditionary Force, with a platoon of fifty-five men under my command. (I am the censor for our platoon so I can write what I like.) We've been retreating towards the River Marne after a bad time at Mons. Some of the men are saying that they saw an angel hovering above them there. If so, I am sure it was a consternated angel, appearing to the Germans as well, and wringing its hands over human folly.

I woke with the thought of you strongly in my mind. I perhaps should be writing to my wife Lulu as this may be my last letter, but I feel compelled to speak to you and explain or apologize for how something went terribly wrong with me.

I should explain about my wife. Yes I did marry after all. I went back to Holland Street after you left, it must have been the summer of 1906. Cornelius said you had gone to Canada and married.

Soon after that I met Lulu, Louise, and we were married within the year. She is a good girl and we have a sort of quiet happiness without tears and trembling.

I assume, and hope, that you are happy. I picture you with children close by, perhaps rosy-cheeked skating on the Canadian ice, hand-in-hand with the good man who is your husband. We have no children.

I still feel this strong tie to you, or at least to my idea of you. I feel compelled to try to explain why I left you so abruptly and to tell you how bitterly I've regretted that over the years. Only now, as I go into battle again, is my heart calm enough to say this: I'm sorry for any hurt I caused. I don't know why things turned out this way. I have let go the bitterness and now hope that if you harbour any bitterness towards me you will let it go too.

This is what happened, my story, for what it's worth:

At the time of our friendship, I was an ardent explorer of a certain mystical way. Now I have become so much less certain of everything and am almost comfortable to be standing here in bewilderment. But then, I worked at everything so hard. I worked at making you love me. I worked at my business of exploring and adventuring. And I worked at the business of trying to become a saint. I was certain that if I worked hard enough I would get whatever I wanted.

I had at the time a teacher who's every word I hung onto and saved and pondered. He was a Persian gentleman who travelled from the East to London on business. You met him once in my apartment. He was a very ordinary looking fellow. Anyone meeting him would not know that he was an initiate of an ancient lineage of teachers. The little man inside me was flattered to gain any attention from him and proud of my association with this esoteric lineage. I was a deluded and dazzled orientalist. How little I understood (or yet understand). I believe it was this proud little man inside who led me astray and led me to make such a terrible mistake with you. I held our lives in my hands, and though the bitterness is almost gone, I remain convinced I did make a mistake for which I have paid dearly and will continue to pay in subsequent lifetimes. But who knows, perhaps all was just as it should be. In fact it must be so. As I say, I sit here in the dawn in complete bewilderment.

Anyway, my dear Mary-Margaret, time is passing and I must continue with my excuses, my apology. That year, when we were so close, my teacher spoke often about freedom, about how so many of us in his little group, the English men he meant, not the Persians, were bound up in illusion and led lives in which Freedom was a word only, dry as dust, an abstraction. We none of us knew what it meant. I hadn't a clue what he was talking about. He said that freedom was real, was available, was incredibly beautiful. I still haven't a clue, though perhaps a glimmering.

When he spoke of freedom in this way, my heart would start pounding. What he spoke of I wanted so desperately. I was hungry for it, but I didn't know what it was. Or the Truth of which he spoke. I still don't have any idea of it but trust that what he spoke of is real. He said that Love is the great energy of the universe and so I still believe.

Now I can almost see your fierce and puzzled eyes. Sometimes I think I see you on the street. In Paris even, where we were going to go together and didn't. This summer before we got into this mess I started to follow a woman who looked so much like you. You would be looking at me with those eyes, encouraging me to continue, questioning my illusions.

My teacher went away. No one in the group knew where he'd gone. I was trying to live out the things he said. Freedom. I became convinced that freedom meant that I should renounce all the things of the flesh, all the conventions of our civilized English life, marriage for example. Somehow this thinking led me to the belief that I should renounce my connection to you.

I was so wrong. If only I had trusted you. My mind twists around trying to find someone else to blame: society perhaps for giving us the idea that women were not able to share everything. For a while I blamed you for accepting my avowal of rejection, for taking yourself away. But I sit here as the mist lifts off the hill across from me and my mind quiets. No one to blame.

A year and a half later, after I had left you, my teacher returned, a businessman who had simply been away selling carpets in another town, so he said. When I told him what I'd done he smiled sadly and shook his head. I understood that I had made a terrible mistake. He said, "Why can't you jut live your life? Why does everything have to be a drama with you?" I went back to Holland Street but you were gone. Cornelius sat with me in his little study and told me that you were married and I understood that I had lost you. I am so sorry.

Now the men are starting to stir. I expect our orders will come in the next few minutes. I have much to do. Though I don't know why I am here, I am, so I will try to do what I have to without dramatics. I suppose it has something to do with my desire to find out what I know for myself, not what my Sheik has told me, or anyone else. I will address this to Holland Street care of Susannah and hope that it will reach you some time. I hope you can read this scrawl. Perhaps we will have another chance in some other lifetime, on some other world. Kiss your children for me.

With abiding Love,

Hugo.

The Modern Age

HOWARD, Mary-Margaret Martin. Passed away suddenly in her sleep on June 3, 1965. Dr. Howard was born in 1880 in Montreal, the daughter of Elizabeth and George Howard. After training at Bishops, she practised medicine and was a beloved family doctor in Vancouver for forty-seven years. She received an honourary doctor of laws from the University of British Columbia in 1949 and the Freedom of the City the year she retired, 1950. Dr. Howard was a member of the Women's University Club and a great proponent of education for women. She loved to travel and after retirement visited South America, Australia, and Mexico. She was a keen and careful gardener and a warm companion to a succession of rascal dogs. She is survived and will be greatly missed by her great-nephew Morgan Howard, his wife Linda, and their two daughters Penny Howard and Sarah Smith. Memorial Service to be held at St. Mary's Anglican Church, Tuesday August 11 at 2 pm. Flowers gratefully declined.

Jane Covernton lives and writes in Roberts Creek on the edge of the Salish Sea in the shadow of Mount Elphinstone. She's written and published two other novels -- *Raindrops and Smoke* and *Cutlass Time* -- and a book of poems *A Body of Poems*.

www.janecovernton.ca